RAGWEED
&POPPY

Read all the adventures of Poppy and friends

Ragweed ★ Poppy ★ Poppy and Rye ★ Ereth's Birthday ★
Poppy's Return ★ Poppy and Ereth

And enjoy these books by Avi

THE BARN

BEYOND THE WESTERN SEA, BOOK I: *The Escape from Home*

BEYOND THE WESTERN SEA, BOOK II: *Lord Kirkle's Money*

BLUE HERON

DEVIL'S RACE

DON'T YOU KNOW THERE'S A WAR ON?

ENCOUNTER AT EASTON

THE FIGHTING GROUND

FINDING PROVIDENCE

THE MAN WHO WAS POE

THE MAYOR OF CENTRAL PARK

NIGHT JOURNEYS

NOTHING BUT THE TRUTH

PRAIRIE SCHOOL

ROMEO AND JULIET—
TOGETHER (AND ALIVE!) AT LAST

THE SEER OF SHADOWS

SMUGGLERS' ISLAND

SOMETHING UPSTAIRS

SOMETIMES I THINK I HEAR MY NAME

S.O.R. LOSERS

THE TRUE CONFESSIONS OF CHARLOTTE DOYLE

"WHO WAS THAT MASKED MAN, ANYWAY?"

WINDCATCHER

~ AVI ~

RAGWEED & POPPY

ILLUSTRATED BY *Brian Floca*

HARPER

An Imprint of HarperCollinsPublishers

ISBN 978-0-06-267134-9 (TR) — ISBN 978-0-06-267135-6 (LB)

20 21 22 23 24 PC/LSCH 10 9 8 7 6 5 4 3 2 1

First Edition

Contents

DIMWOOD
FOREST

LOTAR'S
HOME

THE
CABIN

LONG
MEADOW

TO
AMPERVILLE

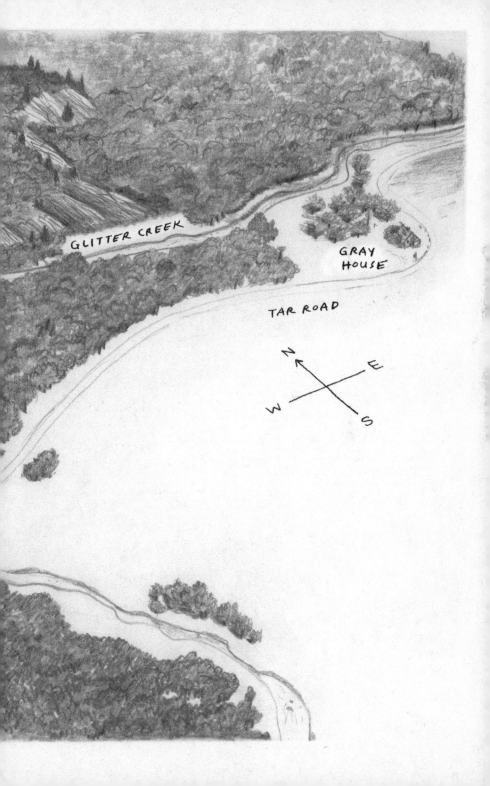

CHAPTER I

Ragweed Wanders and Wonders

WITH MUCH RATTLING, banging, and squealing, the long freight train began to move. Ragweed, a golden mouse with dark orange fur, round ears, and a somewhat short tail, looked out through the open doorway of an empty boxcar. As the world whizzed by, he sighed and brushed away a few tears. One of the tears slid down a whisker and fell with a gentle *plip*.

It had been an amazing adventure: leaving his forest home and family—mother, father, and all those younger brothers and sisters—at the Brook. Getting to Amperville, meeting the female city mouse named Clutch, who was so different, so fascinating. The excitement of the city. Learning the city's language. Struggling with the terrible cats, particularly Silversides. Meeting that sweet mouse,

Blinker. The final triumphant battle against the cats, only to learn that Blinker and Clutch were going to be together and that he, Ragweed, was in the way and that he needed to move on. Though he knew going away was the right thing to do, he felt sad.

Fondly, Ragweed touched the earring—a small purple plastic bead on a short, metal loop—that dangled from his left ear. It was Clutch and Blinker who had given it to him as a going-away present. Thinking of his friends, Ragweed already missed them even as he hoped they were happy.

"I'm not," he murmured.

Was the train moving too fast, or not fast enough? he asked himself. *Hey,* he thought, *I need to be alone, somewhere that'll give me peace and quiet. You're going off to, like, brand-new adventures. But where?*

That brought a new thought: *Am I a country mouse or a city mouse?*

I talk like a city mouse.

I feel like a country mouse.

What am I?

He remembered how, shortly after he left the Brook, he had come to a fork in the road. There, an old vole had told him that one road went east to a Dimwood Forest, the other led to a city. Ragweed chose to go to the city, promising he'd go to that forest someday. "Okay," he said, "someday is today. Forest time."

He lifted his head and, as loudly as he could, sang his family's favorite song:

"A mouse will a-roving go,
Along wooded paths and pebbled ways,
To places high and places low,
Where birds do sing 'neath sunny rays,
For the world is full of mice, oh!
For the world is full of mice, oh!"

Then Ragweed cupped his paws around his mouth and shouted, "Dimwood Forest, here I come!"

Except, he told himself, he didn't know where Dimwood Forest was. Then he remembered the old saying: *if you don't know where you're going, any road will do.*

That thought gave Ragweed some cheer, but not much. He asked himself what he had learned during the dangers he'd faced in Amperville: okay. The best way to stay safe was not to poke his pink nose or toes into other creatures' problems.

"Dimwood Forest." Ragweed said the words again. *Sounds like a place where I can be alone and decide what I am. Cool. A mouse has to do what a mouse has to do.*

As the train sped on, Ragweed worked hard to soothe his gloomy spirits by sitting near the edge of the boxcar doorway and watching the shifting scene: the human houses, cars, trees, flowers, and meadows. They all flew by like windblown leaves even as the train whistled long and low.

An hour later the train began to slow down. With much bumping, banging, and clanking, it came to a stop. Curious to learn why, Ragweed stuck his head out of the boxcar doorway.

Right alongside his train lay another set of tracks. Beyond these tracks was a forest whose green and wildwood fragrance smelled delightsome. *Maybe this is Dimwood*

Forest, Ragweed told himself. *Might as well get off and find out.*

He edged closer to the doorway, braced his legs, and readied himself to leap from the boxcar when there was an explosive burst of air as another train roared by on the parallel tracks, moving so fast it was little more than a blur.

Terribly frightened, Ragweed dived deep into the boxcar. Eyes squeezed shut, taking rapid, deep breaths, body trembling, he put a paw to his chest, wanting to reassure himself that his heart was still beating. It was, wildly.

"Dude," he managed to whisper, "you just dodged being dusted."

Okay, he told himself when he had calmed down, *sometimes doing nothing is better than doing something.*

He crept back to the open boxcar doorway, planted his feet firmly on the threshold, and peeked out. The world was still there. But he didn't even think of jumping out.

Within moments, the train started up and soon regained its former speed. The whistle sounded. The things he had seen before—trees, flowers, human houses, and cars sped by. Then once again, the train halted and Ragweed peeked out. What he saw was a cluster of houses, cars, and people: a human village.

Don't want to be around humans, he told himself. *Too risky. They don't like mice. I need a place where I can't be biffed.*

As the train resumed its rolling rumble, Ragweed realized that his recent scare had made him hungry. He lifted his nose. A scent of something good was in the air.

He peered into the boxcar's depths and only then noticed that in a far, shadowy corner was a rumpled brown paper bag that smelled of food. Scurrying over, he sniffed it. *Something good.* Using his front paws as well as his teeth, Ragweed made a hole. A captivating fragrance wafted out.

Poking his head through the hole, Ragweed saw a piece of bread smeared with thick, nutty, brown paste. The aroma was wonderful and there was nothing Ragweed loved more than nuts.

He scooped up a gob of the paste and tasted it. "Nice,"

he murmured. "The world's best food: peanut butter."

Ragweed settled down and helped himself to a good meal. After stuffing himself he decided to leave the rest for later. *No idea how far I'm going,* he reminded himself. "But this is the coolest way to travel."

Altogether relaxed and well-fed, the steady rocking and rolling of the boxcar made him sleepy. *Nap time,* he thought.

He shaped a hollow on the paper bag big enough for him to curl into. Once there, he snuggled down and closed his eyes. Even as he did, the train began to slow down until once more it came to a full, shuddering halt.

Deciding it didn't matter, Ragweed took a deep breath. "Nuts, nobody, and being nowhere," he said. "Nothing better," and drifted off into an easy sleep.

Moments later, Ragweed heard an irritating scratching noise that roused him from his snooze. Drowsy, he resisted looking. Only when the sound came again—*screech*—louder and much more annoying, did he partially open his eyes.

At first, Ragweed could see nothing. It took the scratchy sound repeating itself a third time for him to sit up and peer about. *What is that?* he wondered. It was when he turned toward the boxcar's open doorway that he saw a small gray paw with five long claws appear over the edge. A second paw with an equal number of claws did the same thing.

A soft grunt came and Ragweed watched, astonished, as an animal heaved itself into the boxcar.

CHAPTER 2

To Whom the Paws Belong

R AGWEED HAD NEVER seen a creature like it.

About the size of a cat, it was covered with dark gray fur, save for its chest, which was white. Its ears were round and slightly pointy. The black nose was sharp, surrounded by white fur and long white whiskers. A swatch of black fur enclosed its dark, bright eyes. That black fur was, in turn, encircled by white fur, so it looked as if the creature was wearing a mask. Its tail was bushy and long, with alternating black and gray stripes. Its forepaws, Ragweed noticed again, each had five claws.

Once the animal had climbed into the boxcar, it sat upon its rump and looked all about as if puzzled by its surroundings, all the while making soft, breathy, and anxious sounds.

What kind of creature is this? Ragweed kept asking himself.

And what's making it nervous? Okay. Remember: do not poke your whiskers into other creatures' lives. So he remained still and watched, hoping the animal would go away.

The animal sniffed a few times. A pink tongue popped out and licked its nose.

Oh-oh, thought Ragweed. *It's hungry. Maybe it wants to eat me.*

The train gave a lurch and began to move, resuming its rapid pace. When it did, the animal whirled about and gazed openmouthed out the boxcar doorway. At first, it seemed to do no more than stare, as if unable to grasp what was happening. Then it let forth a *groan*, suggesting deep misery.

As Ragweed continued to watch, the creature edged closer to the boxcar doorway, lifted one of its paws, and stuck it out into the air. The five long claws seemed to be feeling the passing wind, trying to grasp what it was. Then it crouched back upon its rear legs as if prepared to jump.

Before Ragweed could think what he was doing, he shouted: "Dude, don't do it!"

Startled, the animal looked around.

"The train is going too fast," Ragweed shouted. "Trust me, bozo. If you jump now you'll butter your brain."

"Who's . . . who's talking to me?" stammered the

frightened creature as it gazed around the boxcar in search of the voice.

"Me. Ragweed."

"What's a . . . me-ragweed?"

"A mouse."

"I've never seen a me-ragweed-mouse before. Where are you? What do you look like?"

"Over here, dude. In this corner."

"Can you make yourself bigger?" the animal asked.

Ragweed stood up. "See me now?"

"Is *that* all you are?"

"Sorry," said Ragweed, "mice are small." He cocked his head to one side, touched his earring to reassure himself, and then said, "Mind my asking what *you* are?"

"What do you think? A raccoon."

"What's your name?"

"Lotar." The raccoon studied Ragweed intently but then turned to glance out of the boxcar doorway again, clearly much more concerned with what had happened—that the train was moving fast and the world was speeding by.

To Ragweed's surprise, he saw tears form at the corners of Lotar's bright eyes, tears that began to roll down along his furry cheeks.

"Hey, raccoon," called Ragweed, "what's your problem?"

Lotar stared out of the boxcar doorway. "It's my . . .

mama. She's back . . . there." He made a vague motion with a paw, even pointed with a claw. More tears fell.

"How'd that happen?"

"I was with Mama. *Sniff.* In our rock cave. In the forest. It was all cozy. *Sniff.* She went to sleep. *Sniff.* I did, too, but when I woke up she was still sleeping. *Sniff.* But I was hungry. Only, I didn't want to wake her. Mama loves to sleep during the day. *Sniff.* So I thought I might get a little something to eat. By myself. *Sniff.* And so I went out to find some food and walked a really long time. Through the woods. *Sniff.* After a while, I smelled something good. It was at the bottom of a gully. When I looked down into that gully this huge thing was sitting here."

"It's called a train," said Ragweed.

"Well, I never saw one before. *Sniff.* And it wasn't moving. Not a bit. But I smelled something delicious. And the way was open. *Sniff.*"

"Did it smell like nuts?" asked Ragweed, hoping it wasn't him that smelled good.

"I didn't know what it was," said Lotar. "Except it seemed tasty. And since I was very hungry, I jumped up . . . really high. I never jumped so high in my whole life . . . and . . . got in here. *Sniff.* But then Mama went away." The raccoon lifted his head and howled.

"No," said Ragweed, "you're the one who went away. The train moved."

"Why," asked Lotar with still another *sniff,* "did it do that?"

"It's what trains do."

The raccoon looked back at the boxcar doorway, opened its mouth wide—showing many teeth—and cried, "I want my mama." Tears began to flow again.

"You're awfully big," suggested Ragweed, "to be crying about your mother. How old are you?"

"Two months," said Lotar.

"Okay. Fine. You are a baby."

"That's what Mama says. How old are you?"

"Five months," said Ragweed.

The raccoon studied the mouse. "If I'm younger," he said, "how come I'm bigger?"

This animal, thought Ragweed, *has as much smarts as a splat of spit.* "Hey, excuse me asking; do raccoons eat mice?"

"I don't know. I never saw a mouse before."

"What do you know?"

"I love my mama. And I hate dogs, snakes, and people. Mama hates them, too. She says if I see any of those things I should run away, fast. They bite and it's no fun getting bites."

"Well, your mama isn't here, and I'm not a snake, dog, or people. But your mama is right, keep away from them."

"What's a people?"

"Tall, two-legged creatures, with fur on the tops of their heads," said Ragweed.

As Ragweed studied the raccoon he reminded himself of something: back home at the Brook, his own mama had taught him that he must always look after youngsters. That made him remember his kid brother, Rye. This raccoon was as young.

So he said, "Better come over here and eat something. It'll make you feel better."

Lotar waddled to where Ragweed was. The mouse, all too aware how big the baby raccoon was—compared to him—scooted out of the way. The raccoon sniffed at the bag, and with his two front paws made Ragweed's hole in the bag much bigger. Then he pushed his nose inside the bag, found the food, picked it up with his paws, and began to gobble. As he ate, he made loud chewing noises as well as splutters and gulps.

Though Ragweed was uneasy by how fast this baby raccoon ripped through the bag with his claws, he said nothing. *Better for him to eat peanut butter than eat me,* he thought. "Do you have to make so much noise when you eat?" he asked.

Lotar looked around. "Mama always says that, too."

"Sounds like you need to be told what's going down. And up."

"All I know," protested the raccoon as tears began to fall

again, "is that Mama is gone. Which means there's no one to tell me what to do."

"How about, you know, using your own brain?" suggested Ragweed.

"I'm sorry," said Lotar. "I'm so young I don't have much brain." To prove it he sat down and looked as if he didn't know what to do next.

"Do you happen to know the name of your forest?"

"Dimwood Forest."

"Truly?"

"That's what Mama calls it."

That's when Ragweed had his idea: *this raccoon says he lives in Dimwood Forest. Okay. Maybe if I help him find his mama, I can get where I want to go.*

"Tell you what," said Ragweed. "I'll help you find your mother." Then he added, "Remember, the only one I'm running with is me. When we get you home, put me down as up and out. But if we're going to get there, the first thing we need to do is get off this train."

"You told me I shouldn't get off."

"You can, furball, when the train stops."

Lotar rubbed his face with his claws, then pulled on his whiskers. Tears began to flow again. "But if the train keeps moving . . . won't I keep getting farther away from her?"

"Don't worry, it seems to stop a lot. Next time it does, all we have to do is, you know, get off."

"But . . . then, where would we look?"

"Like you said, in your forest."

"Alone?" More tears.

"With me!" Ragweed shouted. *Be patient,* he told himself. *He's going to get you to Dimwood Forest.*

"What if there are those people in the woods? Or snakes? Or dogs?" said Lotar. "Mama says 'Keep away from them.'" The raccoon put his nose near Ragweed's face again. "Would you, maybe . . . please . . . since you're older . . . and smarter. Could you go first when we look for her?"

Ragweed considered Lotar. *I hope this idea of mine works.* He put a paw to his earring by way of reassuring himself that he was doing the right thing.

"What's that thing hanging from your ear?" asked Lotar.

"An earring."

"What's it for?"

"Something friends gave to me."

"Did you lose them?"

Ragweed, wishing it wasn't so hard to be with an annoying raccoon, said nothing.

"I'll be your friend," said Lotar. "Your best friend. And you can be my best friend."

"I don't want friends," said Ragweed. "Anyway, you're too big."

"That's silly. I'm small. It's Mama who's big. But, when the train stops . . . will . . . you really, really help me find her?" The raccoon pushed his nose right up against Ragweed again. "Extra, extra please."

Ragweed put both paws against Lotar's nose, and with all his strength tried to shove the animal away. The raccoon didn't budge. Gasping for breath, Ragweed said, "Don't you listen? I already told you I would. Now . . . move."

"Thank you," said the raccoon as he pulled back. "I'm going to sleep," he then abruptly said. "Wake me when the train stops. Mouse, I'm glad you're my best friend."

With that Lotar stepped away from Ragweed, lay down, curled himself up into a ball, put his paws over his eyes, and instantly fell asleep.

Ragweed stared at the raccoon. It took him a moment to realize that he was sleeping right on top of the paper bag. *No more food for me.*

He went over to the boxcar doorway and gazed out.

Though it was growing dark he could see they were racing through more woodland. For a moment, he felt the temptation to get away from the raccoon. *But he can lead me to that Dimwood Forest,* he reminded himself.

He walked into a far corner of the boxcar—as far as he could get from the raccoon—lay down, and went to sleep.

Sometime in the middle of the night Ragweed sensed the train had stopped and was now moving in the opposite direction. *Now where are we going?* he asked himself. Then: *Wonder how Clutch and Blinker are doing?* But his last thought before falling back into a deep sleep was: *tomorrow I'll be in Dimwood Forest.*

CHAPTER 3

Getting Off the Train

I<small>T WAS EARLY</small> morning. Bright light streamed into the boxcar, waking Ragweed. He yawned, rubbed his eyes, stretched, stood up, scratched his chin with his left rear foot, smoothed his whiskers and his ears, shook out his tail, and finally, checked his earring. All was in order.

Fully awake, he stepped to the boxcar doorway and looked out. The train had stopped in a deep gully whose walls were covered with bushes and rocks. Above the gully, Ragweed could see the tops of trees. *Maybe it's near the raccoon's forest.* He looked down. Next to the train was a set of parallel tracks.

Hungry, Ragweed peered across the boxcar. The young raccoon still lay asleep atop the paper bag, the bag with the food. *Double dang,* thought Ragweed. *I need to get that raccoon moving.*

"Lotar," he shouted across the boxcar. "The train has stopped. You need to get off before it starts up again or another train comes by. Did you hear me, masked baby? It's getting-off time. Find-your-mother time. Come on. Bang the bustle button."

Lotar, head on the paper bag, eyes closed, remained motionless.

Ragweed went up to one of the raccoon's ears and shouted into it. "Hey. You need to ease up your eyes."

The raccoon continued to sleep.

Ragweed ran around to Lotar's nose and began to beat on it with both paws. "Stripe tail. Wake up."

Lotar slowly lifted his head, partly opened his eyes, blinked foggily at Ragweed, yawned, gave a satisfied sigh, and promptly put his head down and shut his eyes.

"We going to find your mama or not?" Ragweed shouted.

The raccoon's long white whiskers twitched. He opened his eyes. "Hi," he said sleepily.

"If we're going to find your mother," said Ragweed, "we need to get off the train. Now."

Lotar sat up slowly, yawned again, showing his sharp teeth and pink tongue. Then he licked each of his ten claws and used the wetness to poke the sleep from his eyes, one eye at a time. Finally, he said, "I'm hungry. Can you get me some more food?"

"You're sitting on it."

"Oh."

"Raccoon," said Ragweed as Lotar gobbled up the remaining peanut butter and bread, "listen to me. Forget food. The train has stopped. Which means this is your chance—maybe your best chance for the rest of your life— to jump off and find your mother. You know, rip and run."

Lotar looked at Ragweed quizzically. "I forgot your name," he said.

"It's Ragweed." Ragweed ran to the boxcar doorway. The train was still not moving. He gestured out. "Bustle, baby. Leap before we lose it."

The train let forth a long, shrill whistle.

"Hear that?" shouted Ragweed. "It's saying what I'm saying: *move*."

Lotar lumbered to his feet, swung about to sniff at the paper bag, and then waddled over to where Ragweed was waiting by the boxcar doorway. "What do I do?" he said.

"Do?" cried Ragweed. "What do you think? Like, jump out of this boxcar. Totally. Off. Out. Fast. Now. Did I say that simple enough?"

The raccoon shook his head. "I don't know how to jump off a train. I've never done it before."

"It's easy," said Ragweed. From the boxcar edge he looked out, and thought up a plan. He'd jump off first, then get the raccoon to follow.

"Okay," he said to Lotar. "Watch what I do. Then, you know, do the same thing. Any questions? I'm going to leap off now. Easy. Watch me."

The train whistle blew again.

"Remember," cried Ragweed, "you *must* follow me."

Lotar stood by Ragweed and peered down to the ground. "It's a long way," he said.

"Dude," said Ragweed, "guess what? The only way to get off a train is to get off."

Lotar, staring at the ground below, shook his head. "It's too far."

"You got on, didn't you?"

"I was going the other way."

"Okay, raccoon, watch what I do."

With that, Ragweed leaped out of the boxcar. With a
soft *plop*, he
landed on a
spread of loose
gravel between
the parallel
iron rails. He
looked up.

Lotar peered
down at him from
the boxcar doorway.
"Are you all right?"

"Course I am. Come on. Hit the hop."

"It's too far."

"It is not far," called Ragweed. "You have to do it. Jump."

"I'm scared," Lotar called, putting his paws before his
eyes.

"You don't have to do anything but drop," Ragweed
shouted up.

"What if I hurt myself?"

The train whistle shrieked.

"Raccoon," said Ragweed, "if the train starts up, and you're still on it, you'll never see your mama again."

Alarm filled Lotar's face. "If I jump will you catch me? Mama always does."

"You're too big for me to catch."

"But . . ."

The train gave a lurch. Couplings clanged and banged.

"The train is going," cried Ragweed. "Jump."

"Is it going toward Mama?"

"Doesn't matter. Quick."

"I'm scared."

The train picked up speed.

Ragweed ran alongside the moving train. "Raccoon, this is your last chance."

The train went faster.

"I want my mama!"

Ragweed was racing as fast as he could alongside the moving boxcar. "Dude," he screamed up at the raccoon, "if you ever hope to see your mama again, get off the train, *now.*"

Lotar shut his eyes and leaped.

CHAPTER 4

In the Gully

HAVING LANDED ON his belly, the raccoon lay there.

"I did it," he cried. "I got off the train. Did you see me, mouse? I flew through the air. Like a bird."

There was no response. "Hey, Ragweed-mouse," cried Lotar. "Where'd you go? Did you leave me?"

Not moving, the raccoon looked around. The train was gone. And there was no sign of Ragweed. "Did you go back on the train?"

Lotar listened hard. All he heard was a tiny muffled "*Uff*," but couldn't grasp where the sound came from. He continued to lie there.

"Mouse," he called. "I hope you didn't go away. You're my best friend."

There was no reply, although Lotar felt an uncomfortable tickle on his belly.

"*Uff,*" came the small sound again.

Lotar felt a sharp pinch. "Ow," he cried, leaped up, and looked down. There, on the pebbly ground, lay Ragweed.

"What are you doing there?" asked Lotar.

"Dude, you landed on top of me."

"Oh, sorry. I didn't mean to. That was the first time I ever flew. I haven't learned to land yet. Really," said Lotar, "you're my best friend. In fact, you're my only friend. Except for Mama, but she's not a friend, she's my mama. Which is much better. And you're going to find her. Thank you. I love you. We'll never leave each other again. Best friends forever." He bent over and gave Ragweed a wet lick.

Saying nothing, Ragweed pushed himself up, wiped the raccoon's spittle off his face, and stared down the tracks. The train was out of sight.

Ragweed turned to consider Lotar. "Seriously," he finally said, "I only want to help you find your mother. You're much too big to be my friend."

"If you think I'm big, wait till you see Mama," said Lotar. "She's huge. Much bigger than me. The strongest raccoon in the world. But sometimes," Lotar added in a whisper, "she gets mad at me."

"No kidding," mumbled Ragweed. He stared down the empty tracks, thinking, *I have to get rid of this raccoon.*

"Come on," said Lotar. "Let's go find Mama." He clapped his paws together and put his face close to Ragweed. "I'm the baby. You're older and smarter. My best and only friend. So, you're in charge. Okay. Let's go. I'll follow you back to Mama."

Ragweed gazed down along the gully where the tracks ran. It was steep—with many woody branches growing out of it. He looked up. Above the gully, he could see treetops. "Fine," said Ragweed, "That's forest up there. It's where you came from, right?"

"Maybe."

"For starters," said Ragweed, "you need to get out of this gully. Being on these tracks is not, you know, safe. Once you're up there—in that forest—we can start looking for your mama. Follow me."

Without further ado, Ragweed started to climb, all but running up from the gully bottom, scooting from rock to rock, between branch roots, climbing outcrops. Once he reached the top he looked back below. Lotar was still sitting on the tracks at the bottom of the gully.

"Come on, raccoon," cried Ragweed. "Get up here."

Lotar tried to follow Ragweed, but every time he climbed some, he tumbled to the bottom. He did this five times. After the fifth time, he sat back, looking befuddled. Sitting between the train tracks, he peered up at Ragweed who was gazing down at him. "I can't do it," he cried.

"How'd you get down?" asked Ragweed.

"I fell down. Do you know what? I think you should come down here and push me up."

"Impossible."

"Can you pull me up?"

"No way."

"I have another idea."

"What?" said a frustrated Ragweed.

"I'll wait here. You find Mama and tell her to come here. She's a whole lot stronger than you. She'll get me up."

"Raccoon," cried Ragweed, "I have no idea where she is. Besides, waiting down there isn't smart. If a train comes you'll be popcorn pieces."

Lotar became alarmed. "Will a train come?"

"I don't know. But it'll be a whole lot safer if you were up here."

The raccoon didn't move.

Ragweed leaned over the gully edge and looked up and down along the tracks. Not far along to the right, the gully appeared to flatten out. If Lotar went there, Ragweed decided, he should be able to get out of the gully with ease.

"Walk down that way," he called, pointing. "You'll be able to get out. I'll stay up here. Now, flick your fast switch forward."

With that, Ragweed began to walk along the top edge of the gully. Lotar, down below, followed, ambling along inside the railroad tracks. Ragweed continued to gaze at the tracks, up and down. Sure enough, in the far distance, in the direction they were heading, he saw something. He stopped and stared.

"Hey, baby-brain," Ragweed cried, "another train is coming this way."

"Where?" cried Lotar, instantly full of panic. "Where should I go? I don't see it. Is it going to hurt me?"

"Raccoon, you need to get out of there, fast. Double down on the upswing."

"Which way. Up? Down? Sideways? Help!"

"Move it, or you'll never move again in the worst way."

Full of fright, Lotar reached high, grabbed a branch growing out of the gully wall, pulled himself up, all the while shoving desperately with his rear legs.

"That's it," cried Ragweed, keeping an eye along the track. The train was coming along swiftly. "Faster."

Unnerved, the raccoon continued to grab whatever he could and moved higher.

As the approaching train drew closer, a shrill warning whistle shrieked.

"You're doing it," cried Ragweed. "Keep coming. Don't slide back."

Lotar clutched branch after branch while kicking with his back legs until he reached the top of the gully. Once there, Ragweed took hold of the raccoon's claws, clung to them, and pulled back with all his strength.

The raccoon came up and plopped over the lip of the gully. Down below, the train roared by. As the ground trembled, Lotar squeezed his eyes shut, clapped his paws over his ears, and breathed rapidly.

What followed was nothing but a dusty silence.

Lotar remained still, eyes shut. "Mouse?" he whispered. "Am I . . . am I still alive?"

"Dude, you made it."

Lotar opened his eyes and looked all around. "Wow," he said. "You know what?"

"What?"

"I'm the bravest raccoon in the world. First I jumped down, then I climbed up."

An irritated Ragweed said nothing, only turned around to see where they had come. On one side was the gully and the train tracks. On the other side was nothing but trees.

Ragweed waved toward the forest. "Does any of this look familiar?"

Lotar sat up and looked around. "Sort of."

"What part?"

"The trees."

Ragweed sighed. "How about describing where your mother lives?"

"There are all these big rocks. Piled on one another so it makes a kind of hole. We live in that hole that is dark and cozy. That's all I know."

"Try smelling. Does your mother smell?"

"She sure does," said Lotar. "I love her smell. It's sweet and warm." He lifted his nose and sniffed. Once, twice, three times.

"Anything?"

"That way, maybe."

Ragweed went in among the trees. Lotar shuffled after him.

Stay in charge, Ragweed told himself. *Find his mother. That should get you near Dimwood Forest. Now, boom your bones and rip the road.*

CHAPTER 5

In the Forest

LOTAR FOLLOWED RAGWEED among the forest trees. Ragweed could see only a little sky. It was all a cool, green dimness. Grasses were low, bushes were tall, the ground soft and sweet smelling. He did hear birds, but it was hard to see them. There also was the sound of insects chirping and clicking, altogether a bustling buzz.

Abruptly, the raccoon stopped.

"What is it?" asked Ragweed. He had been thinking about how nice it was to be back in the woods.

"You're going wrong. I bet Mama is that way."

Ragweed sighed. As Ragweed headed in a completely new direction, he thought: *How much longer?*

A few moments later Lotar sat down under a large tree. Frustrated, Ragweed waited. The raccoon remained silent for a long while. He scratched his nose. Opened his mouth. Shook his head. "Guess what?" he said.

"What?"

"I have no idea where Mama is." He tilted his head back and wailed, "Mama! Come find me!" He began to cry.

Ragweed looked up at the weeping raccoon. *Never again,* he told himself, *should you offer to help anyone. Ever. Being alone is the only way I'm going to find out who I am.*

Even as they sat there a pine cone dropped, barely missing Ragweed's head.

"Barfing baboons in bug butter" came a sharp voice from above. "What's all that racket?"

Ragweed and Lotar looked up. Over their heads, where a branch joined the tree trunk, a large, bristling gray porcupine was looking down at them. His teeth were yellow. His prickly tail was swishing about in great agitation. In his long claws, he held another pine cone.

"A forest is supposed to be quiet," the porcupine snarled. "Or did you forget to glue your ears to your heads when you woke up this morning?"

"It's this raccoon," Ragweed called up. "He's a baby. I'm trying to help him. He's lost his mother."

"That's the trouble with this world," said the porcupine. "Kids have no respect for parents. Losing your mother is nothing but carelessness." To make his point the porcupine dropped the pine cone. Ragweed dodged it.

"If this raccoon has lost his mother," the porcupine went on, "he needs to find her. Do it fast and without all this feathered fish fuss. That's what I say." He dropped another pine cone. It hit Lotar, but other than blinking, the raccoon didn't seem to notice.

Ragweed called up: "Can you tell me where we are?"

"You're standing under a tree."

"Dude, all I see are trees."

"Creatures who say 'Dude' are dung beetle doughnuts. There are trees because this is a forest. It's called Dimwood Forest."

"Delighted to know it," said Ragweed. He called up. "Now, have you seen any raccoons around?"

"I'm a porcupine. I don't like raccoons. In fact, I don't like anyone and no one likes me. So lift your leaky legs and lug yourself somewhere else."

"It's this baby," persisted Ragweed, pointing to the raccoon. "He says his mother lives in a big pile of rocks. Is there anything, you know, like that around here?"

"Why should I tell you?" asked the porcupine. "Because if we knew where those rocks were, we could haul fast and leave you alone."

The porcupine flicked his tail

back and forth, try-
ing to decide if he
should reply. Finally,
he said, "There's a whole pile
of rocks about half a mile that way." He
pointed. "Now go away. Skunk stink soda.
I need quiet."

"You got it," said Ragweed. "Come on, Lotar. Triple trot."

"Don't ever come back," the porcupine yelled after them
as the two animals moved away. "And my name is Ereth,"
he mumbled. "Not that anyone cares."

Ragweed, still in the lead, walked through the woods
in the direction the porcupine had suggested. *Guess I got to
Dimwood Forest,* he thought to himself. *Nice.* Behind him,
moving slowly, Lotar toddled along. *Now, all I need to do is get
rid of this raccoon. . . .*

"Did that animal in the tree tell you where Mama is?"
the raccoon asked.

"Hopefully," said Ragweed.

"Guess what?" said Lotar. "Even when you find her I'm
going to be your best friend forever and ever."

Under his breath, Ragweed whispered, "Dude, you will
never see me again." He pushed on, desperate to find that
pile of rocks so he could get away and be alone.

~ CHAPTER 6 ~

A Pile of Rocks

"ARE WE GETTING there? Are we close?" asked Lotar five different times in five different ways as he trotted along behind Ragweed. "I'm getting tired. Can we take a rest? I'm hungry. When can I eat? How long will it be before my mama finds me? Can I take a nap? Can't you go slower?"

Ragweed, refusing to answer any of Lotar's questions, trudged on, constantly standing on his rear toes in search of the pile of rocks. All he saw were endless trees, tall grasses, and yellow dandelions; no boulders. "These rocks better be somewhere soon," he grumbled.

"What did you say?" asked Lotar.

"Nothing," said Ragweed.

"Please find Mama," said Lotar. "I'm getting tired. I really need a nap."

"Keep coming," Ragweed shouted.

The two continued to plod on through the forest. As they went along, the young raccoon kept stopping to pick a flower, or snatch up a bug, or carefully examine a leaf, while constantly asking Ragweed about what he found. Ragweed returned short, blunt answers.

"Do you have to pick up everything you see?" Ragweed asked.

"Only the pretty things," said Lotar as he carefully plucked up a snail and offered it to Ragweed. "I got this for you."

Ragweed shook off the gift and kept moving forward, feeling increasingly discouraged. *What am I going to do,* he asked himself, *if I can't find his mother?*

But it was not long after that Ragweed spied a heap of gray boulders piled one on top of the other. He stopped. Standing up on his hind legs as tall as he could, he stared at it, hoping it was what he was looking for, Lotar's home. At the lowest level, there was a dark hole. That seemed promising. "Hey, pal," he called back to Lotar. "Is that it? Your home?"

Lotar stood up and looked. "Yes," he cried. "That's it. My house. Mama," he shouted. "I stopped being lost. You found me." He rushed forward.

Ragweed stepped out of his way.

A huge raccoon—big, bulky, and powerful-looking—burst out from within the rocks. Four feet long, her white whiskers were bristling, her rump was high, and her striped tail was thrashing about furiously while her black eyes glittered with anger. As she emerged, she gave a loud yowl, her wide-open mouth showing many sharp teeth, in particular, two fangs.

Terrified, Ragweed shrank down.

Lotar, however, rushed right up to the big raccoon and hugged her front leg.

"Mama," he cried. "It's me, Lotar. I got hungry but you were asleep so I went away all on my own and then I fell into a gully and got on what's called a train and the train went fast but a very smart Ragweed-mouse found me some food and I was brave so I jumped off the train and ran right up a gully and we went through the forest where a grumpy old porcupine told us which way to go but he dropped a pine cone on my head except it didn't hurt me and so we came and here I am and this Ragweed is my best friend in the whole world. He took me."

"Took you?" cried the mama raccoon. "Were you kidnapped?"

"What does kidnap mean?" asked Lotar.

"Someone took you."

"Oh, yes. My best friend here took me."

"What kind of friend is that?" demanded the mother raccoon, glaring furiously at Ragweed.

"He said he was a Ragweed-mouse. Did I make a mistake? Was I supposed to eat him?"

Ragweed, trying to make himself as small as possible, had crouched down. Cautiously, he stood up and allowed the big raccoon to see him. He waved a paw and offered a friendly smile. "Nice to meet you, ma'am," he said.

Lotar's mother peered at him. "This tiny mouse *took* you?"

"He did," said Lotar. "He really did. He's my best friend forever."

"He's not a friend if he *took* you," cried the large raccoon and she rushed toward Ragweed.

Ragweed didn't know which way to go.

"Take my boy, will you," cried the raccoon and opened her mouth wide.

"No," cried Ragweed, hastily backing up. "You don't understand what happened. He was totally lost. On a train. I was, you know, trying to help him. So I took him here. To you, his mama, to you."

"You have no right to take him anywhere," snarled the raccoon. "You can take yourself somewhere else, thank you."

With that, the big raccoon reached down and, using one of her paws, gathered up Ragweed in her claws, and with all her strength, flung the mouse as far away as she could. At the same time, she let forth a loud, angry growl.

As Ragweed flew through the air he heard Lotar cry, "Mouse. Come back. Don't worry! You're my best friend forever. I'll come find you. I will. I promise I will."

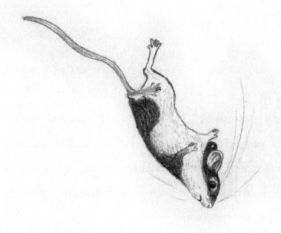

CHAPTER 7

In Dimwood Forest

R AGWEED SHOT THROUGH the air in a high arc only to drop atop a clump of yellow dandelions. That allowed him to land sweet and soft, with nothing more than a sneeze from the dusty pollen that exploded into the air like a golden cloud. Sliding to the ground, he shook his head clear, only to hear one more—but distant—yowl from the angry mother raccoon.

Ragweed began to run through the woods, not caring the slightest where he was going. As long as he was getting farther away from Lotar and his mama that was good enough for him. *See,* he scolded himself, *keep your nose out of other creatures' business.*

Tired of running, he stopped, sat down, and listened. The forest that surrounded him was altogether quiet. No more snarls from that big raccoon. No more calls from

Lotar that he was going to look for him.

"They're gone," said Ragweed. "I'm gone. Gone is good."

He put a careful paw to his earring, making sure he hadn't lost the purple plastic bead. Relieved to find it still there, he took a deep, satisfied breath, and gazed about at the forest.

"Well," he whispered, "still must be Dimwood Forest. I made it."

The light in the forest was faintly misty. A mass of trees—some with thick, knurly bark—reached great heights. Higher still were patches of blue sky, with willowy wisps of white clouds. Younger trees, small, slender, and kelly green, grew closer to ground. As for the earth, it was carpeted by tall grasses and tufty bushes, as well as old brown leaves, which gave a sweet-smelling scent of gentle decay. Amidst fallen branches and logs, a clump of pale blue columbines had grown. Old logs were bearded with green moss and shelves of brown mushrooms. Soft breezes teased the air. All was quiet save the random chirp and peep of invisible birds.

"Is this where I belong?" Ragweed whispered in a quiet voice, feeling it wrong to speak loudly. Still, other than knowing the name of the forest, he had not the slightest notion where he was.

Realizing he was hungry, he looked about. He noticed a few pine cones on the ground not far from where he sat. He picked one up, peeled back the scales, and plucked out a seed. "Plenty of good food," he said.

Ragweed sat there, chewing the seed with satisfaction, utterly content with this soft, secluded world.

As he looked about, he reminded himself, *You are totally nowhere. Maybe nowhere is the best place to be. Okay, I've reached Dimwood Forest. Now what? And where?*

Since he didn't know where he wanted to go—other than away from the raccoons—he decided to let the wind decide.

He plucked a blue petal from a flower and threw it into the air. A gentle breeze floated it off to the right. "Fine," said Ragweed. "I'll go that way."

Feeling free and utterly calm, Ragweed ambled along, enjoying the forest. *Nice. Extra nice.*

It didn't seem to matter how far or how long he walked, the wildwood seemed to be the same even as it was endlessly different. Now and again, he paused to eat one of the tasty seeds he found along his way or to drink some fresh dew that had gathered in a flower. "This is good," he fairly chirped. Softly, he sang the second verse of "A Mouse Will A-Roving Go."

"A mouse will a-roving go,
By highways, byways and long wooded trails
To forests; cities. Rain or snow,
Not bothered by cats, or the smallest snails
For the world is full of mice, oh!
For the world is full of mice, oh!"

Ragweed continued to walk for some time until unexpectedly he came upon a rutted dirt road. Seeing tire tracks, he stopped. *Oh-oh,* he thought. *A human road.*

He gazed up and down the lane. It looked deserted. Nothing passing to worry him. Nor were there any troubling sounds. Wondering where the road led, Ragweed moved along its edge, threading his way among the grass.

The road made a sharp turn out of the forest and onto a meadow. Ragweed had come to a bright, wide, and rolling field. In contrast to the forest gloom, it was filled with a great array of tall and short grasses, plus low bushes in full leaf. The sky above was blue, with a few drifting clouds. White-bellied swallows dived and swerved, gulping bugs on the fly. Bumblebees lumbered through the air, moving from white flowers to golden ones, from golden ones

to pink ones. Orange-winged butterflies fluttered lazily by. A grasshopper, its wings rattling and showing a streak of yellow, leaped up only to land a few yards away.

"Different but nice," Ragweed said as he continued to follow the dirt road.

After moving on a little farther, Ragweed saw what appeared to be a car. That stopped him. At first glance, the car looked like the one that his friend Clutch lived in back in Amperville. It only took seconds for him to realize that it wasn't *that* car.

Clutch's car had been a rusty brown, with some pieces removed, along with soft wheels that sank halfway into the ground. This car was a shiny blue—new and clean—with fat wheels entirely visible. Besides, Amperville had to be miles away.

Still, seeing the car caused Ragweed a painful pinch of memory: he missed his friends. But, most importantly, as far as Ragweed was concerned, a new car meant that people were likely to be near. That could be unsafe.

He hesitated. *Should I run off, or see what's going down?*

Curiosity won. Ragweed crept forward, making sure to stay clear of the car, all the while watching it intently. He had gone a little farther on when he spied—beyond the

car—a human nest: a house. That stopped him again. He studied it.

The building stood alone in the meadow, under the shade of the forest. It was not anything like the human houses he had seen in Amperville. Not only was this one isolated, but it was rather small, and made of logs stacked neatly one upon another. Ragweed also noted a few small windows and a door. The door was shut.

Ragweed gazed at the house, trying to determine if anyone was inside. Nothing was moving. Then he heard laughter and human voices. No question: people were inside the house.

Oh-oh, Ragweed told himself, *snatch yourself some space.*

Even as Ragweed took a step away, the door to the house opened and three humans emerged. The people were of different sizes; a tall one, a small one, and a middle-sized one. Ragweed watched them.

"Susan," called one of the bigger people. "Jump into the car."

The small person ran to the car, opened a door, and climbed in. The other two followed. Then they, too, got into the car.

There was a loud roar, and a stink filled the air enough to make Ragweed wiggle his nose.

The car rolled backward, then swung about in a half circle.

Ragweed sprinted off the road, but stopped and watched.

The car proceeded to move slowly down the lane, past Ragweed, and then rolled on into the forest, in the opposite direction from the way he had come. It was soon out of sight and sound.

Good, Ragweed told himself. *They're gone. I don't want anything to do with anyone.* "Now, lift your legs," he muttered, "and get away." But he had barely taken one step when he heard a voice crying:

"Help! Will someone please help me?"

CHAPTER 8

The Cry for Help

RAGWEED STOOD STILL.

"Please," the cry came again. "I need someone, *anyone*, to help me."

Trying to discover from where the call was coming, Ragweed stood on his hind legs as tall as he could and looked about.

"Help me, anybody."

The voice seemed weak and weary. *Someone's in trouble. At least it doesn't sound like Lotar.* That was a relief. Even so, Ragweed, unsure what to do, stayed where he was.

"Please," the cry came again, sounding a little weaker, a little sadder.

Do I want to help anyone else? Ragweed asked himself. He thought about everything that had happened in

Amperville. He thought about helping Lotar. He thought: *What if those humans come back?* It seemed likely they would. *I don't think I should stay here.* As he tried to make up his mind what to do, the call came again, even more mournfully: "Will someone, *anyone*, come and help me."

Ragweed was now sure the appeal was coming from the back of the log house. More importantly, he was also certain the caller was a mouse.

He felt embarrassed. *How can I stand here and do nothing?* he scolded himself. *That's, you know, wrong.* He sighed. *If it's a mouse that's in trouble, I have to help.*

With extreme care, Ragweed crept around to the back of the log house, moving in the direction of the pleading voice. Upon turning the corner of the house, all he saw at first was a plot of cut grass and some faded yellow and red flowers. Then he realized that right next to those flowers, on the grass, was what appeared to be a box.

It was an odd box.

No more than ten inches long, and three inches in height, the box was shiny silver in color. And seemed to be made entirely of metal. On the box was writing:

HAVAHART
LITITZ PA

While the thing was surely box-like, it was full—on all sides—of small square holes, through which Ragweed could see inside. It was, he realized, something like a cage. Most important of all was what Ragweed saw inside the box: a mouse.

The mouse had a plump, round belly, which was white-furred, although the rest of the body fur was orange brown in color. The ears were large. It did have full whiskers and the nose was small. There were also delicate pink toes and a tail that was longer than Ragweed's.

"I do wish someone would help me," said the mouse from within the box. It was that same tedious, exhausted voice Ragweed had heard before and seemed to be speaking to no one in particular. "I don't care who it is," called

the mouse in the box. "Come and help me."

To Ragweed's ears, the request sounded as if the mouse had given up any hope that anyone would come, but felt, all the same, compelled to ask.

Guess I'm the one, you know, who came, thought Ragweed, not pleased by the fact.

Though Ragweed was now standing in the open, the mouse in the box didn't appear to see him. Belatedly, Ragweed realized that the mouse had its eyes closed, as if asleep or exhausted. He edged closer and studied the mouse. When he did, he realized he was looking at a deer mouse such as ones he had seen at Clutch's music club in Amperville.

Ragweed continued to watch while the deer mouse

poked listlessly at the holes on the side of the box as if trying to get out. But since the holes in the box were small and close together, Ragweed was certain it was impossible to get through them.

Then Ragweed also realized that at each end of the box were metal flaps. These flaps were folded down, like shut doors. There were also some rods sticking out alongside the box, but he didn't know what they were for.

"Oh well," he said and drew closer. "A mouse has to do what a mouse has to do. Hey, dude," he called out. "What's happening?"

With a start, the deer mouse opened its eyes and peered out through the holes. Those eyes were round, dark, and glistening with tears.

"Oh, thank goodness," cried the mouse. "I'm *so* glad to see you. Will you *please* help get me out of here? I've been trying for so long but I can't."

"How about getting out the same way you got in?" suggested Ragweed.

"I wish I could," said the deer mouse. "But . . . the holes are too small and it's shut up tightly at both ends. I'm afraid . . . this is"—the voice wobbled with a sob—"a trap."

"A trap," cried Ragweed, only now fully understanding what the metal box was.

"And," said the deer mouse, "it's closed up. Tight."

"How'd you get in?"

The deer mouse sighed. The furry cheeks even seemed to turn slightly pink. "I hate to admit it, but I wasn't paying attention to where I was going. I mean, to tell the truth, I . . ." The mouse seemed hesitant to speak. "I'm afraid I . . . I . . . well, I sort of, I guess, wandered in here."

"*Wandered into a trap?* How'd you manage that?"

"You see, before—when I came upon it—both ends were wide open. So I . . . walked in. I must have tripped on this metal flap. It must be kind of a switch. Because the doors—at both ends—crashed shut. The most horrifying sound I ever heard. Ghastly. That's when I realized that . . . I'd gone into a trap and when you get into a trap it's . . . it's . . . hard to get out."

"You telling me you didn't look where you were going?"

"My . . . my eyes were closed."

"Closed!"

With an uncomfortable shrug, the deer mouse made a little nod.

This, thought Ragweed, *is a seriously bit-brained mouse.* "How long you been in there?" he asked.

"A whole day and night. There was a piece of something to eat in here. But I ate it a long time ago. Which means I'm hungry. And thirsty."

Ragweed looked around and spied a few seeds on the

ground. He gathered some up, went up to the trap, and slotted them through one of the square holes. The deer mouse snatched them up and ate rapidly, pausing only to say, "Thank you. You're most kind," and then went back to ravenous eating.

Ragweed found a flower with dew in it. He brought it to the side of the trap. Inside, the mouse made a cup with two front paws. Ragweed poured the water in. The trapped mouse lapped it up eagerly.

"Thank you again," the deer mouse said, sitting back with evident relief.

"There's a human house here," said Ragweed. "That where you live?"

"Oh no. Not at all. But I haven't seen any people."

"I saw some."

The mouse gasped. "You did?"

"Afraid so. Three of them. Big, too."

"When? Where?"

"A short while ago. On the other side."

"Oh dear," said the mouse in the trap. "I was sure that it was people who put this thing here. Maybe to . . . catch mice. I was hoping they were gone but scared they'd come back and find me in here. When I considered what might happen . . . it . . . it could be . . ." The mouse was unable to say the words.

"Yup," said Ragweed, "bad to the bone."

"Are they . . . are they still . . . near?"

"They went away," said Ragweed. "In that car. Didn't you hear it? A roaring and a stink."

"I did wonder what that noise and smell were. I'm afraid I'm not thinking clearly. I'm so hungry, and terribly worried."

"Thing is," said Ragweed, "I'm sure they'll be back. But, mind my asking, if you don't live here, where do you live?"

"On the far end of Long Meadow. That way." The deer mouse pointed in an easterly direction. "It's not that far. But too far for any of my family to hear me calling."

"How big is this family of yours?"

"Oh . . . maybe two hundred and fifty."

"Think anyone, you know, would come and rescue you?"

"Oh, yes. My mother always says, 'Mice should be nice.' Mostly, I think we are. They'll help, I'm sure they will. The problem is, they have no idea what's happened to me. Do you think you could get me out? I so want to go home."

Inwardly, Ragweed groaned. *Someone else to help.* But he felt ashamed to have even had that thought.

"Please," the mouse in the trap fairly begged.

"I can try," said Ragweed. "By the way, what's your name?"

"Poppy."

CHAPTER 9

Helping Poppy

To which Ragweed said, "Okay, '*Poppy*.' Pleased to meet you."

Poppy grasped the bars of the trap with her two front paws and peered out through the holes. "Thank you. May I ask, please, what's your name?"

"Ragweed."

Poppy said: "I don't think I've ever seen a mouse like you before. But I have to admit, I've never traveled far from home. Your tail is a bit . . . short. You're not a deer mouse, are you?"

"Golden mouse. Is that, you know, a problem?"

"Oh no," said Poppy. "Not at all. I mean, your fur is nice. And, anyway, I don't care what you look like. I'm so happy to see you. I've been in here so long, I was beginning

to think no one would come. That I might even . . . die here. Do you live nearby?"

"Nope. Way away. But we need to like, chop the chatter, try to get you out."

"Thank you. It is awful in here. Have you ever been in a trap?"

"Nope. Don't intend to, either. I, you know, like to keep my eyes open. Okay. Let's see what I can do."

The first thing Ragweed did was grasp the metal bars around one of the holes with his two front paws, and give them a few shakes. They didn't budge. Then, using more strength, he tried to pull the bars apart and make a bigger hole. That didn't work either.

"I tried all that," said Poppy.

The next thing Ragweed did was go to one end of the trap, where the sheet metal flap had closed down. He attempted to lift it. It would not move. He struggled again, pulling as hard as he could. The flap stayed put. He went to the other end of the trap, and attempted the same thing, but achieved no more.

Finally, he tried to pull at the side rods. That didn't make any difference either.

Returning to where Poppy was looking out at him, he said, "Sorry, can't seem to open anything."

"I tried pushing those flaps, too," said Poppy, sounding almost apologetic. "I think they're locked. I don't know how."

"Let's try it together," suggested Ragweed.

The two of them attempted to pull apart the bars and then went on to try to lift the end flaps. Nothing moved.

Ragweed sat back and looked at Poppy. "Not sure what I can do," he admitted.

"I don't want to be here for the rest of my life," said Poppy. "But if those humans come back . . ." She shuddered visibly. "I might not even have a life."

"I get it," agreed Ragweed. "Not gleaming good. Now, you said you have a big family. And you think they would help."

"Oh, yes," said Poppy. "The minute they know what happened to me I'm sure they would come."

"Cool," said Ragweed. "Then I'll hurry on over, tell them what's happened and where you are. With a whole pack of paws, you know, they should be able to flip these flaps. You good with that? Tell me again where you live. You said it was close."

"Oh, yes, thank you. You'll need to go through Long Meadow. But make sure you don't go into the forest. I never do."

"Why not?"

"It's dangerous. All kinds of awful creatures live in there. Anyway, once you cross through the meadow, you'll reach a creek. We call it Glitter Creek. Walk along its bank until you see—on the other side—an old orchard. That's the best place to cross. It's narrow there. Even so, the creek is deep in places, so you'll need to stay on the rocks to get over.

"Once you get over, go through the orchard and past an old pump. After that, you'll come to a human house. We call it Gray House. It belonged to someone called Farmer Lamout but no humans live there now. But I should tell you, lately, some people have been coming around. We don't know why. It's worrying. Everyone is tense. That was one of the reasons I wanted to get away for a bit. My papa has been extra irritable lately. As it is, he doesn't like out-siders. He might not be welcoming.

"Anyway, that's where I live. Gray House. Lots of my

family should be around. As I said, I'm sure they'll come as soon as they learn what's happened to me."

"I'm on it," said Ragweed.

"Oh," said Poppy, "another thing. Make certain you don't go beyond Gray House. If you wander across the Tar Road or up Bannock Hill, you've gone too far. It might not be safe."

"Is there any place that's safe around here?" asked Ragweed.

"Well, not . . . completely."

"Never mind. I can, you know, handle it. Now, tell me again, how far is this Gray House?"

"I can't say precisely. Not too far." Poppy pointed. "It's that way. I promise. Oh," she continued, "when you get there, it would be best if you spoke to my father first. His name is Lungwort. He's in charge of everything. You can't miss Papa. He always wears a thimble on his head. My mother's name is Sweet Cecily. They're the ones you need to ask. Except . . ."

"Except what?"

"I'm afraid my father . . . like I said, doesn't like strangers."

"Hey, we just met each other," said Ragweed. "I know your name, Poppy. You know mine, Ragweed. So we're not strangers anymore, right?"

"That's sweet of you to say," said Poppy.

"Okay. Let me go hustle," said Ragweed. "Hold on. I'll get you some more food and water." He scurried about and gathered up as many seeds as he could find, and dumped them through some holes into the trap. Then he pushed through a small cup-shaped flower, found some dew, and poured that in.

"That should work until your family gets here," said Ragweed. "I'll go as fast as I can."

"What should I do if the humans come?"

"You need to ask? Hide."

"But . . . where?"

"Anywhere."

Poppy looked about. "I'm afraid there's not much room to hide."

"Then make yourself as small as possible. In a corner. Don't say anything, either. Hey, if you want my advice, from now on, you know, keep your eyes open."

"But . . ."

"Okay, I'm heading out. I don't expect we'll see each other again. I've got places to go. Things to see. Good luck."

"But—"

Ragweed, however, was already gone, running in the direction Poppy had suggested.

Clutching the bars of the trap, Poppy looked after him.

Thank goodness he came, she thought and sat back. *What was his name? Oh, yes, Ragweed.*

I should have told him: I was pretending to be a dreamy ballroom dancer when I went into the trap. My parents don't approve of dancing and I never got permission to go. Just wandered off by myself. The trouble with wandering is, you can get lost. But with those humans coming around Gray House . . . I needed to get away.

Poppy sighed. "Dancing is such a nice feeling. The grass is so gentle on my feet. The air soft. When I close my eyes, I feel all . . . whirly. It's . . . it's as if I were in the center . . . the exact center of the whole world. But I wasn't, I was in this trap."

Then Poppy became aware that there was another thing she should have told Ragweed: yes, the forest was dangerous. But it might be as unsafe to go through Long Meadow. All kinds of bad creatures lived there, too.

Oh, I do hope nothing happens to him. That would be awful. I could never forgive myself.

With that troubling thought, Poppy went off to a corner of the trap and tried not to think what might happen if those humans returned.

Even as she settled down to wait, she shuddered and whispered, "Hope that Ragweed gets to Gray House fast."

CHAPTER 10

The Real Estate Agent

HANDYMAN'S SPECIAL

Old farmhouse. Handyman's Special, but fixable.
Three bedrooms. One bathroom. Good water well.
Large rooms. Many closets. Two acres. Beautifully
situated next to an old apple orchard, full flowing
creek, and access to Dimwood Forest. Commuting
distance (forty miles) to Amperville. Owned by High
Prairie Bank, which wishes to sell. Immediate move
in. All reasonable offers considered. Call: Amperville
Real Estate. 555-3367. Ask for agent Jack Sonderson.

CHAPTER II

Across
Long Meadow

Ragweed plunged into Long Meadow, running in the direction Poppy had told him to go. Once out on the big field, he hesitated.

Here I am, he thought, *helping someone again. But, like, I couldn't simply leave her, could I? She's in a bad place. And a mouse has to do what a mouse has to do, right? I'll just tell her family where she is, that she needs assistance, then take off.*

Ragweed hurried on, but couldn't stop thinking about Poppy. *Walking into a trap with her eyes closed,* he mused. *Not the sharpest spice on the kitchen shelf. Still, she was nice.*

Since bushes and tall grasses were everywhere, Ragweed had to pause every few feet, stand up on his hind legs, and study the way forward, constantly hoping to catch sight of what Poppy had called Glitter Creek. Not seeing it, he continued on until he came upon a short-grassed, open plot that was flooded with warm sunlight.

Better to be careful than clipped, Ragweed reminded himself and stood as tall as he could at the edge of the clearing and studied it. That's when, right in front of him, Ragweed saw something moving about in the grass. He stood still and stared hard, trying to determine what he was seeing.

At first, all he could tell was that some creature was thrashing about furiously. Even so, it didn't seem to be going anywhere.

Unable to see with any clarity, but not wanting to get too close to whatever it was, Ragweed spied a bush that overlooked the clearing. He scurried over, climbed up, parted some of the bush leaves, and looked out over the grassy area.

What he saw made him gasp.

It was a snake, a long, thick, light brown snake with dark bands, an arrow-shaped head, and a blunt nose. Its red, forked tongue kept popping in and out of its mouth, like an unsheathed dagger.

Merely to see the snake made Ragweed's blood turn cold. *Dude,* he reminded himself, *snakes eat mice. Swallow them whole. Even that silly raccoon hated them. Nobody likes them.*

As Ragweed watched, the snake coiled around and its head rose up and down, pointing here, then there, as if sniffing out something. Suddenly, the snake stopped shifting about, and—Ragweed had no doubt—aimed its eyes directly at him. They were dark, disturbing eyes, almond shaped with black pupils—hardly more than narrow slits. Terrifying.

A trembling Ragweed—as though under a spell—could not take his eyes from the snake. *Does it see . . . or smell . . . me?* Scared, he held his breath and remained motionless.

The snake extended its head toward Ragweed, seemed to smile, and hissed sweetly, "I sees you."

Ragweed was too petrified to reply.

"And," continued the snake, "I wish some simple support." The snake used words with lots of *s*'s, as if continually hissing.

"Me?" Ragweed managed to whisper. "Were you talking to me?"

"Yesss. Who else? I wish you to seize my tail and secure it in your pawssss."

"Your . . . your tail? W-why do you want me to do that?" stammered Ragweed.

"I'm seeking to shed my sssskin, and seek some assiss . . . tance."

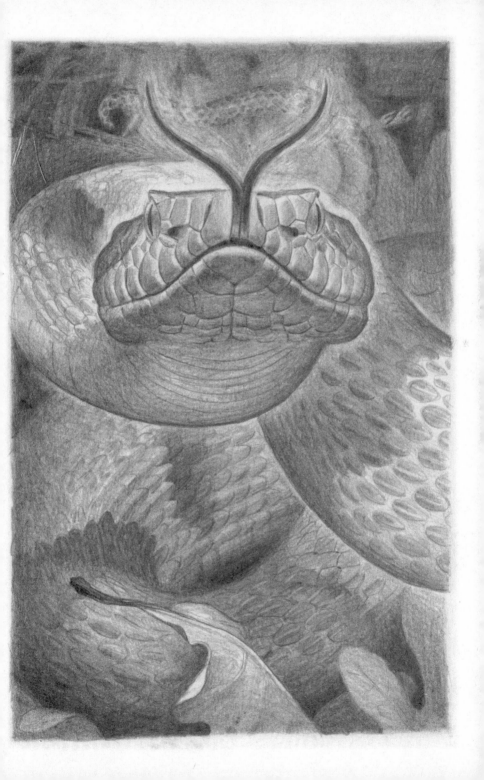

"Don't you . . . eat mice?" asked Ragweed.

"Well, yesss," said the snake. "I do, sometimesss. But not thissss time. I'm simply searching for some ssssupport so I can slip out of my skin. It's seemssss to be a little ssssticky."

The snake glided nearer, but never took its unblinking eyes from Ragweed. "Please, step clossser," commanded the snake.

You've no choice, thought a trembling Ragweed as he climbed down from the bush, aware that although the snake had now stopped moving, its eyes followed his every step.

As soon as Ragweed drew near, the snake coiled about and presented its tail.

"So far ssso good," said the snake. "Pleasssse, grasssp my tail ssssecurely."

Ragweed took the snake's tail into his two paws and tried to get a firm grip, which was hard because he was shaking so.

"G-got it," he said. "Now what?"

"Sssstay serene, but ssssimply grasp my tail with all your strength," said the snake and he began to wiggle about with great liveliness.

Ragweed had to struggle to hold on to the tail.

In moments, to Ragweed's astonishment, the snakeskin slid away and seemed to become a second snake. Except this new snake, though long, had no motion of its own. It was the first snake that moved away from the second snake, spun around, and faced Ragweed. As his tongue slipped in and out, the snake smiled.

"Thanksssss so much," said the snake. "My fresssh skin feels silky and soft. So nice. See youssss. Have a sweet spring day." With that, the snake slithered among the tall grasses, slipping from Ragweed's sight.

As for the snakeskin, it remained in place and lay motionless upon the grass.

Ragweed stared at the discarded skin. *What happened?* he asked himself. *Is that thing alive or dead? Did the snake become two snakes?*

With utmost care, Ragweed crept forward—ready to run away—toward what the snake had left.

Coming as close as he dared, and still uneasy, Ragweed looked all about. The snake was completely gone. He turned back to the skin. Gradually, he realized what he was seeing: nothing more than a cast-off skin. The living snake had wiggled completely out of its old one. The danger was gone.

Ragweed took a deep breath and moved closer to the discarded skin, gingerly putting out a paw and poking it. Nothing happened. The skin lay there, a long, thin, and hollow tube.

"Creepy weird," said Ragweed. "It's like, you know, a banana sliding out of its own peel."

Ragweed was still standing there, fascinated by the skin, when he heard someone shouting: "Ragweed. Where are you? I need you to come back."

Ragweed recognized the voice: it was that exasperating young raccoon, Lotar.

CHAPTER 12

Who Called

"Double dang and dirty," said Ragweed. "That bubble-brained baby raccoon has come after me." In haste, he looked about, saw a thick clump of tall grass at the far edge of the clearing, and darted into its midst. Once there he pried apart some stalks and peered out.

Lotar burst out of the bushes. Rushing into the middle of the clearing, he stood up on his hind legs and looked all around.

"Ragweed!" he called. "Where are you? It's me, Lotar. Your best friend. I'm really sorry my mama threw you away. I want to play with you. Where did you go? Are you near?"

Ragweed stayed hidden.

Lotar took a few more steps forward when he suddenly spied the snakeskin. He halted and goggled at it. "Yipes," he cried. "I think it's a snake." He raced off into the meadow until Ragweed lost sight of him.

Ragweed waited, wondering where the mother raccoon was. He was sure she would be close behind. Sure enough, the big mother rushed into the clearing.

"Lotar," she called. "Come back. Do you hear me? Right now. I want you to stop. It's time for your nap."

When Lotar did not return, the mother raccoon continued to lumber after her youngster. "Lotar, listen to me. I want you to come back. Now." On she went until she, like Lotar, was completely out of sight.

Ragweed gazed after them. *Raccoons, porcupines, traps, snakes, and people,* he thought. *How did that Poppy ever get across all this? Were her eyes closed all the way? She's either a lot stupider or braver than I thought.*

Making sure that the raccoons were going in a direction different from the one he wanted to go, Ragweed dashed across the clearing and continued going across Long Meadow.

"Get yourself to that Gray House," he mumbled. "Tell them about Poppy, and then get your tail somewhere else."

Yes, he thought as he continued running, *get absolutely, quickly, totally, finally, out of here.*

CHAPTER 13

Glitter Creek and Gray House

MOVING AS FAST as he could, Ragweed continued running through Long Meadow. It didn't take long before he came upon a rapidly moving creek. Its bright waters were tossing and turning, with a constant splash and burble, frothing up small pillows of white foam. Ragweed had little doubt it was what Poppy had called Glitter Creek. The name certainly fit. But at the place where he had reached the flowing water, it was too wide, and probably too deep to cross.

He scurried on, moving along the moist bank until he found a place where the creek seemed narrowest. Sure enough, beyond the water, he could see what appeared to be an apple orchard. Ragweed recalled that Poppy had mentioned that. Looking farther on, Ragweed could make out an old human house, which, he supposed, was where

Poppy's family lived: what she called Gray House.

It was all as Poppy had told him.

Almost done, Ragweed told himself.

But first, he needed to cross the creek.

He surveyed the flowing waters. The creek was some seven feet across, still far too wide and rapid for him to swim across. For all he could tell the waters might be deep here, too. But the creek was tumbling around numerous wet and moss-covered rocks that poked up through its surface. Poppy had been right. To get across he would have to leap from rock to rock.

He studied the stones with care, plotting a path across. It would require—he decided—some fifteen jumps. Most hops

looked easy. One or two might be a stretch. He was confident he could do it.

He took his stand at the creek's edge, close enough so that the water tickled his front toes. Tensing his leg muscles, he took a bound and landed squarely on the first rock. Barely pausing, using his momentum to help, he jumped again and secured his footing on the next stone. On he went, leaping from rock to rock. On the tenth, he landed poorly, wobbled, almost fell, but managed to steady himself by holding his front paws wide to the side and his tail straight behind him. *Steady, steady,* he told himself. To his relief, he kept his place and did not fall.
He went on. Within moments, he was on the far side of the creek, safe.

Cool, he told himself. *I'm good. Hey, nothing I can't do. Almost there and out of here. Next stop, that orchard. Go, dude.*

He hurried on, wending his way among the apple trees, all of them old and twisted. Berry bushes were plentiful, as were many different flowers. Overhead, different kinds of birds flew about.

Decent place, thought Ragweed.

Once beyond the orchard, he passed a rusty water pump on a concrete pedestal. Then, right before him, stood the house, which he could have no doubt was a human nest. Looking as if it was about to collapse, it hardly seemed a place that humans would live.

The roof—which had many shingles missing, and with other shingles as curly as late autumn leaves—drooped in the middle, with both ends higher like the bowed back of an old horse. As for windows, only a few had glass. The rest had empty spaces. One window was filled with dust-coated cobweb threads. Nor could Ragweed see a door, simply an empty frame on an uneven porch, which in turn was surrounded by a warped railing. The building's wood-sided walls were a dull gray.

Great mouse house, Ragweed acknowledged. He also had little doubt this was where Poppy's family lived, the one she had called "Gray House."

Belatedly, he noticed that a small red flag was sticking out from one of the roof ends. He wondered what that meant.

He also noticed that beyond the house, on the side of the road, was a red-and-white sign:

HOUSE FOR SALE

Amperville Real Estate
Call: Jack Sonderson
555-3367

Ragweed saw no humans. But he did see mice, a large crowd of them milling about in front of the house. At a glance, he could see that they were all deer mice—like Poppy—and they were playing, eating, and talking to one another with constant squeaks and chatter.

Ragweed considered the crowd and thought, *If these mice are as nice as Poppy said they'd be, telling them about her troubles shouldn't take long and she'll get quick help.*

Boldly, Ragweed marched forward, now and again

pausing to stand tall so he could see and be seen. But as he approached the house and was noticed, the crowd of mice stopped everything they were doing and in complete, stony silence watched intently as he drew near. It was as if a hundred eyes were fixed on him. The only thing that moved was their noses, which quivered as if smelling him, and not at all caring for the smell. Not one mouse spoke, much less called out an openhearted greeting. Nor did he

see so much as a gesture of friendly welcome.

Ragweed was taken aback. This was not a friendly reception. *I thought Poppy said these mice were nice. Something's not right.*

He drew nearer and then called out, "Yo, dudes."

Not a single mouse replied. Instead, they continued to

stand perfectly still and stare at Ragweed as if he were the strangest creature they had ever seen. *This is not*, he thought, *an openhearted place.*

Standing still, he had half a mind to turn about and walk away. *Goodbye, Poppy. Nah. They need to, you know, learn about her.* So, he waited, hoping someone would come forward.

After a few painfully long, silent moments—during which time the crowd of mice merely gawked at him—an old, skinny mouse with droopy gray whiskers and tired eyes stepped forward. He did not come close. "May I help you?" he said stiffly.

To Ragweed's ears, the way the words were spoken seemed to say, "I don't want to help you."

Nonetheless Ragweed held out a paw. "The name is Ragweed."

The old mouse kept his distance. After a few stony, soundless moments, he said, "May I ask; what kind of mouse are you?"

"Me?" said Ragweed, surprised by the question and putting a paw to his chest to make sure the old mouse was talking to him. "I'm a golden mouse. Why are you asking? You have, you know, some problem with golden mice?"

"I don't believe I've ever seen your kind before. Are you from around here?"

"Nope."

"Where then?"

"Back there . . . somewhere. By the Brook. Not exactly sure where. Too complicated."

"I see," said the old mouse, and his unfriendly face made it clear he did *not* see. "And may I ask," the old mouse went on, "what brings you to Gray House?"

"Dude," said Ragweed with growing annoyance, "I'm bringing a message from someone who said she lives here."

"And whom might that be?"

"Calls herself Poppy."

"Poppy," cried the mouse, showing emotion for the first time. Moreover, the name caused a stir among the crowd of gawping mice, bringing much whispering among them as Ragweed heard Poppy's name being repeated over and over again. Obviously, they knew her.

"Well, yes," said the old mouse, "Poppy. She has been missing for a few days. We've been worried about her. That's why we put up the red flag. Have you any idea where she is?"

"She's been caught in a trap, a human trap."

"A trap." That word was also repeated—with considerable alarm—among the mice. Some of the mice even drew closer to Ragweed, as if now wanting to hear what he might say.

"Is Poppy hurt?" asked the old mouse.

"No, but she can't get out of the thing."

"And—where is she?"

Ragweed, frustrated by all these questions—which lacked friendliness—made a waving motion. "Down by that long meadow that runs alongside of the forest. I can tell you where. But how about, like, instead of questions, you gather up a gang and go get her free."

"I'm afraid we don't do things that way," said the mouse. "You'll need to speak to Lungwort first."

Lungwort, Ragweed remembered, was Poppy's father.

"Talk to anyone, pal," said Ragweed. "Except I think you might want to ratchet up the rescue. She's not bunking down in what I'd call a bubble bath. No saying what might happen."

"What do you mean?"

"There are humans where she is."

That stirred the crowd of mice anew.

"There have been humans visiting here," said the old mouse. "Are they the same ones?"

"No idea," returned Ragweed.

"For your information, my name is Plum," said the old mouse. "Please, follow me. I shall take you to Lungwort." He waved a paw and the throng of mice divided in two, leaving a narrow lane for passage.

Amidst silent, inquisitive, and even hostile stares, Plum

led Ragweed down the constricted way, across the cluttered and crowded porch of Gray House, through the open doorway and inside a large room. Once there, Ragweed saw many more mice. When he appeared, they, too, stopped whatever they were doing and stared at him. Some of the outside mice came up and stood by the doorway and peered in as if wanting to see what was going to happen.

Surrounded by all these unfriendly mice, Ragweed felt more and more awkward.

Call me done and deal me out, he thought.

"This way," said Plum. He led Ragweed past an old straw hat and then up to a large, shabby farmer's boot that lay on its side. In front of the open end of the boot was a striped curtain made from a plaid necktie, the kind humans wear.

Plum pulled the curtain aside and shouted down into the boot. "Stranger here to see Lungwort! Says he knows where Poppy is!"

He turned to Ragweed and in a grave voice whispered, "You'll have to speak to Sweet Cecily first."

"Who's she?"

"Poppy's mother."

"Oh, yeah, right. I'm cool. I'll talk to anyone."

The curtain shifted and a mouse poked her head out from inside the boot. It was Sweet Cecily.

She was a small mouse, with soft, pale, half-lidded eyes.

As she looked out from the boot she considered Ragweed with distaste, then flicked an ear with one of her paws. It seemed to be a gesture of unease. "Yes, Plum?" she asked softly. "Have we received some news about Poppy?"

"This mouse," said Plum, "says he knows where she is."

Sweet Cecily regarded Ragweed for a long moment, all the while flicking an ear. She did not smile. "Who," she finally asked in a whispery voice, "are you?"

"Name's Ragweed. I was strolling along the forest edge when I came across Poppy. She's your daughter, right? Anyway, I'm guessing she's one of them. Thing is, she's caught herself in a human trap and can't get out. And, you

know, that thing is as nasty as a nest of needles."

"Oh dear," said Sweet Cecily as she flicked her ear. "I wouldn't know anything about that. How did Poppy ever do such a thing?"

"Said she wandered in."

"Wandered." Sweet Cecily made a clucking sound. It was a small sound, but it struck Ragweed's ears like big criticism. "That's so like Poppy. I'm afraid she doesn't always look where she's going. Lately, we've been visited by humans so that's hardly wise. We're worried they might come and live here."

"No idea," said Ragweed. "All I can tell you is that Poppy

worked to set herself free, but couldn't. I tried to help. Not enough paws. So she asked me to come here so that a gang of you—you are family, right?—could help. Get enough and you should be able to spring her out. No big problem."

Sweet Cecily continued to gaze at Ragweed as if she found it hard to absorb the news. Then she said, "You'll have to speak to her father. Lungwort. He's the one that manages this family."

"Hey, I don't care who I speak to," cried Ragweed, increasingly exasperated. "Only it seems to me you need to shake the dust, hit the road, and pound a path so you can do some heavy lifting. That is if you want to pop Poppy. Get my meaning?"

Sweet Cecily studied Ragweed with wide-eyed bewilderment but made no reply, other than to flick an ear. Then she said, "What kind of mouse are you?"

"Golden mouse. Hey, how come you all keep asking that? Does it matter?"

"We don't see strangers often. It's always wise to be careful. And now, with those humans lurking about—"

"Just trying to help," Ragweed interrupted.

"Hmmm. Come along. Lungwort is our leader. He always knows what to do." With those words, Sweet Cecily pulled the curtain aside and beckoned Ragweed to follow.

CHAPTER 14

Poppy Waits

Back by the log house, from inside the trap, Poppy had watched Ragweed run off into the meadow. *Oh,* she thought, *thank goodness that mouse showed up. He's so nice to go to Gray House. As soon as my family knows what happened to me, they'll hurry and get me out of here. I know they will.* "Please come soon," she whispered to the air.

As Poppy tried to settle down, she felt both better and worse: better because she knew help was coming; worse knowing it would be a while before that help arrived.

Understanding that she had no choice other than to wait, Poppy decided it would be wise to follow Ragweed's advice: make herself as small and still as possible. Accordingly, she gathered up the seeds he had left, ate some, took a sip of water from the flower, and then wedged herself into a far corner of the trap, the place where one of the end flaps came down at a sharp angle.

Be patient, she told herself as she made herself as comfortable as possible. *That mouse—what was his name?—Ragweed, he'll be back as soon as he can.* "He will . . . he will," she kept chanting under her breath. "He absolutely will." The rhythm of her yearning soothed her.

But as Poppy continued to sit, she began to feel annoyed. The problem was, she hardly knew where to direct her anger, at the trap or herself.

"No," she made herself say. "It's not the trap's fault. It's *my* fault. Dancing with my eyes closed. That wasn't smart."

Bored and restless, Poppy got up and tried to do what she had done before, spread the holes in the trap sides wider so she could escape. When she couldn't budge them, she worked anew to lift the end flaps. She had no more success there than before.

"Be patient," she scolded herself anew as she settled back into the corner. "That golden mouse will come back as fast as possible. And he'll bring the whole family. I bet a hundred will come. I'm sure they will."

After a while, Poppy fell into a doze only to be woken by loud noises, first a roar and then an odd squeal. Instantly awake, she listened intently. The sounds ceased. When she peered out of the trap she saw nothing to alarm her. But when she sniffed, she did catch a foul smell. She guessed what the sounds and the smell meant: the car Ragweed had told her about had returned. Sure enough, there were some banging noises followed by human voices.

The people had come back.

Poppy thought about the humans who had been reported around Gray House. She hadn't seen them, only heard about them. Not knowing who or why they were there, they had made all the mice upset. She knew humans had once lived in Gray House. What if they returned? The thought came to her: were these returning humans the same ones that had been to Gray House?

Heart pounding, she wedged herself as tightly into the corner as possible. To compose herself further she closed her eyes.

All was silent. But then, though her eyes were still closed, Poppy heard something close; a scuffling and a scratching. She had no idea what caused it.

She opened her eyes and was shocked to see a gigantic girl's face right outside the trap. The brown eyes on the face seemed enormous, and they were looking right at her.

Poppy realized that the trap was being lifted into the air.

The whole world seemed to slide and bounce. Next came sounds of running and a human voice shouting: "Mommy. Daddy. Look. I caught something in the trap."

The girl carrying the trap—with Poppy inside—rushed into the log house. As for Poppy, all she could think was, *What's going to happen to me?*

CHAPTER 15

Poppy's Father, Lungwort

As Sweet Cecily, Poppy's mother, stepped along inside the boot, Ragweed followed. The boot was shadowy, narrow, and airless. It also smelled of old leather. Walls were covered by rough cloth. Only a bit of light came from a couple of small windows that had been chewed through the leather.

You're almost done here, Ragweed reminded himself, eager to be away from these unfriendly mice and to get back to the open road once again. *The only thing worse,* he told himself, *than helping helpless creatures is helping unfriendly helpless creatures.*

Sweet Cecily stopped and made a beckoning gesture to Ragweed. He came forward and peered into the gloom. At the far toe end of the boot, a portly mouse sat on a bed made from white milkweed fluff. His paws were clasped across his bulging belly, and his eyes were closed as if lost in deep thought—or sleep. Ragweed wasn't sure.

Though the mouse's fur was a bit scruffy, and his front teeth stuck out a bit, his whiskers were carefully curled. On his head was a thimble, which looked something like a crown.

He's asleep, thought Ragweed, hearing the slight rumble of a snore. *These mice keep their eyes closed too much.*

Sweet Cecily approached the fat mouse timidly. "Lungwort," she whispered. "Here's a stranger who says he knows what happened to Poppy."

There was no response from the thimble-headed mouse.

"Lungwort?" Sweet Cecily coaxed.

Lungwort opened his eyes. When he did, he stared down—blinking—at Ragweed without saying anything.

Ragweed, not sure how to react, gazed back and waited impatiently.

"Lungwort," repeated Sweet Cecily, "this mouse says he has news of Poppy."

After a few more moments, with some mild coughing and clearing of the throat, Lungwort spoke: "Now, what kind of mouse are you?"

Ragweed sighed. "Hey, Pops, I'm a golden mouse."

The mouse, still sitting, drew himself up a little taller. "I beg your pardon," he said. "What did you call me?"

"Pops. Aren't you Poppy's old mouse?"

"I may be Poppy's father but I am *not* old. And do not call me 'Pops.' It's vulgar. You may call me by my proper name, Lungwort. Now, then, where do you come from?"

"Some ways from Dimwood Forest. Place called the Brook."

"Then you've traveled far from your home. Why would you ever do such a thing?"

"Hey, Pops, a mouse has to do what a mouse has to do."

"I think it's wiser for a mouse to do what he's *told* to do," Lungwort retorted. "What is that . . . that *thing* dangling from your ear?"

"An earring."

"Odd," said Lungwort. "What is it *for*?"

"Kind of a memory."

"Of what?"

"A city."

"Are you a city mouse or a country mouse?"

"Not sure."

Lungwort frowned. "And your name?"

"Ragweed."

"Ah," he said knowingly but didn't share his knowledge. Then he said, "And how did you come to meet Poppy?"

"I was cutting a cruise alongside the forest—the other side of your creek. Not going anywhere in particular, seeing what I could see, when I heard someone calling for help. Turned out, it was Poppy. Your daughter, right? She was in a trap. A human one. And the trap was shut. Totally tight."

"A *human* trap?" said Lungwort. "Are the humans who put it down the same ones we've seen about here?"

"Dude, I don't know anything about that."

"I'm not surprised," said Lungwort, "that Poppy should come to be in such a dreadful predicament. She's far too independent. She sets a bad example."

Deciding he had better not say anything about Poppy having her eyes shut as she entered the trap, Ragweed said, "All I know is that's where she is. Stuck. Can't get out. The two of us tried to free her, but it was like cracking a nut using feathers. We couldn't do it. You guys need to put some paws to your jaws. Know what I'm saying? Less talk, more traveling.

"Anyway, she suggested I come here and get help. Said you were nice and you would. But the bad thing is that the humans—I don't know anything about the ones hanging around here—the ones who probably put the trap down— they might come back. So you either send some help today or your daughter might be only yesterday. Get my meaning?"

"I do *not* get it," said Lungwort. "Where is this trap, precisely?"

"Dude," cried Ragweed, growing ever more exasperated, "I told you. Across that creek. Down along the meadow. Out by the side of that Dimwood Forest."

Lungwort turned to Sweet Cecily. "Did Poppy have permission to go there?" he asked.

"I don't think so."

"Typical," said Lungwort. "Not asking permission to go places causes problems and is exceedingly precarious. Particularly at a time like this."

"What time is it?" asked Ragweed.

"Humans have been coming here. It's troubling. If one mouse goes off on her own, it weakens us all."

"Whatever," said Ragweed. "But I'd suggest you gather say, at least a dozen or so and go out to where she is, and you know, open the trap. But fast."

"A *dozen?*" echoed Lungwort, making it seem like a vast number. "This is not the right moment."

"Hey, I could tell them where to go," Ragweed offered. "Like I keep saying, and you don't seem to hear me; you need to hurry."

"I shall consider the matter," said Lungwort. "You are a golden mouse. We are deer mice. May I suggest we do things differently. We consider things with care. I am constantly warning my household: avoid porcupines, people, raccoons, and strangers. We are cautious."

"Hey, Pops, cheese the cautious. You either rescue your daughter or not."

"I'm not going to endanger the whole family for one mouse. Besides, it's not for you to tell me what to do, young stranger. As I told you, we have big problems with which to deal.

"Now, you have my permission to leave. Goodbye." He turned to Sweet Cecily. "Please show this . . . boy out. And," he called after his wife, "now that we know where Poppy is, have them take down the red flag."

"But—" Ragweed started to say.

"Goodbye," Lungwort said again. With that, he tapped his thimble hat, folded his paws over his belly, and closed his eyes.

"This way, please," said Sweet Cecily. She scurried down along the boot, pausing only to make sure Ragweed was following.

A frustrated Ragweed stayed with her.

Once he stepped beyond the boot, Sweet Cecily looked out and said, "Young fellow, I think you had best go back to where you came from. We much prefer to be with our own." With those words she closed the curtain, leaving Ragweed alone.

"Bummer," said Ragweed. "It doesn't seem like they're even going to look for Poppy. *Mice should be nice,* he remembered Poppy saying. *Well, these mice aren't nice. Guess I better move on.*

CHAPTER 16

Cousin Basil

Ragweed looked around. Any number of deer mice were standing about watching him but keeping their distance, not speaking. It was almost as if they were scared of him.

Ragweed touched his earring. *I can't open that trap,* he told himself. *Not alone. Not even with Poppy. But these mice don't seem to care much about her. Nothing else I can do. I should get out of here. Poppy will have to take care of herself. Come on, dude,* he told himself, *beat your feet.*

He headed for the doorway of Gray House and had almost reached it when a young mouse stepped in front of him. He was a small fellow, with spindly legs, short whiskers, and pink eyes.

"Hello," said the mouse, holding out a paw in a friendly fashion.

Ragweed, pleased to meet someone who was welcoming, shook the offered paw.

"My name is Basil," said the young mouse. "Poppy's cousin—twice removed. She and I are good friends. I've been worried about her. The word going around is that you found out where she is."

"Right, she's in a trap."

"A trap," cried Basil. "Where?"

"Somewhere out there. Along that meadow. By Dim-wood Forest."

"Is she all right? What kind of trap? A human one? How'd she get into it?"

Ragweed told Basil about Poppy's predicament.

"How'd you ever find her?" asked Basil.

"Wandering," said Ragweed.

"Thank you so much," said Basil. "But forgive me, do you mind telling me your name?"

"No, sure. Ragweed. But, hey, I don't get it. You mice don't seem to be friendly. Or want to help Poppy."

"You were talking to Lungwort, weren't you? And before that to Plum."

"Who?"

"Tall, skinny old mouse."

"I guess."

"I'm afraid we haven't been welcoming. Everybody's worried about the humans who have been hanging around Gray House. It's all we're thinking and talking about. We're guessing it's about that sign some human stuck up by the side of the road. Every time the people show up we have to hide in the closets. It's annoying. And worrying. We don't know what's happening. Might be the most crowded home in the world, but it's our only home."

"I hear you," said Ragweed.

"Let's go on out to the back steps," suggested Basil. "No one will be there. We can talk. Can you take the time?"

Ragweed, not comfortable with Gray House, wanted to get the talk over quickly so he could resume his travels. *But if he could help that Poppy* . . . "Okay," he said.

He allowed Basil to lead the way out through the back of Gray House where there was a small porch and steps leading down. The two mice sat on the top step.

"I suppose," began Basil, "I should begin by apologizing. See, we've been living here for a long time. You might have already noticed; it's far too packed. We need another place. But the truth is we don't even look elsewhere. Or go anywhere. Or do anything. We're not allowed to. All we do is stay here. That means we're not used to outsiders. And Lungwort is our leader. But I suppose having more than a hundred children is a big responsibility."

"Glad I'm not one of them," said Ragweed.

"He is grumpy. Thinks a lot of himself. And as I told you, those humans . . . Anyway," continued Basil, "the point is, if we do go anywhere away from Gray House, we have to get Lungwort's permission. Which is hard to get."

"Why do you need permission?"

"Mostly," said Basil, "it's because of porcupines."

"Porcupines," cried Ragweed, remembering the bad-tempered creature he met in the forest. "What's wrong with porcupines?"

"I'll tell you some other time. I need to hear about Poppy."

Ragweed described the trap Poppy was in and where it was. Thing is," he concluded, "that food and drink I gave her, it won't last long."

"That's bad," agreed Basil. He shook his head. "It's unusual for any of us to go behind the creek. How come she went?"

Ragweed, unsure if Poppy would want to share her story, once again decided not to tell how she went into the trap, with her eyes closed.

"All I know is," he said, "it'll take, you know, a bunch of you to open the trap. Only thing, those humans—the ones who put the trap out there—might come back."

"What do you think they would do to her?"

Ragweed shook his head. "I can think of all kinds of stuff and most of them not nice."

"Okay," said Basil. "Tell me again where she is."

Ragweed waved in the direction of the forest. "Like I said. Out there. Along that meadow."

"Can you be a little more specific?"

"I don't think so," admitted Ragweed.

"If I round up enough mice," said Basil, "and I think I could, would you be willing to lead us back to where she is?"

"Not sure I want to."

"Why?"

"Most of you mice don't seem to want me here."

"I am sorry about that. Thing is," said Basil, "it would be a whole lot faster if you led us to where she is."

Ragweed touched his earring, which made him remember Clutch and Blinker. He missed them. "I've sort of got my own travels to do," he said.

"Where to?"

"Not sure."

"There's no way we'll be able to find her on our own," pressed Basil. "Not quickly, and you said it has to be. How many mice do you think it'll take to free her from that trap?"

Ragweed could hear himself saying, *Come on, dude. A mouse has to do what a mouse has to do.* Then he said, "It would take, you know, nine, ten."

"I can round up that many," said Basil. "Only thing, I have to be quiet about it. Can't let Lungwort know. We'll sneak out. And if you lead us there we could rescue Poppy fast. Would you, please?"

In his thoughts, Ragweed had to admit they would

never find Poppy on their own. The meadow was too big. Reluctantly, he said, "Fine. But, know that, soon as I show you where she is, I'm going to head off. You know. Done and drifting."

"Fair enough," said Basil. "Give me a minute. Wait here." Basil hurried back into the house.

Left alone, Ragweed sat on the steps, heaved a small groan, and then repeated to himself what he had told Basil: *Okay. Soon as we reach Poppy, I'm done. On my way. Totally. I mean it, too. This time totally total.*

─ CHAPTER 17 ─

The People

THE GIRL CARRYING the trap—with Poppy inside—
rushed into the house and set it on a table. Poppy, shocked
by what had happened, worked to make herself as small
as possible. Even as she did, she couldn't help give a moan
that was equal parts disappointment and fear. *A human,* she
thought. *It can't get worse.*

But it did. Within moments, there were *three* humans
sitting around the table and all of them were staring right
at Poppy.

"What kind of animal is it?" asked the girl, the one who
had carried Poppy inside.

From inside the trap, Poppy peered out. It was as if this
human had a head but no body because her chin was resting on the tabletop, the better to see her. The girl's smiling
face fairly glowed with excitement.

"It's a mouse, Susan," said the largest of the humans. He had a low voice, and he did not sound pleased.

"Certainly, a mouse," said the other human, the middle-sized one. "But we should look it up and find out what kind it is. There are many kinds."

"It's so cute," said Susan. "Can I keep it? Can I? Can I bring it back home?"

"I don't know," said the deep-voiced human. "Most times, sweetheart, people prefer to keep mice *outside* their homes."

"Why?"

"I'm afraid they're dirty," he said. "And they carry disease. To tell the truth, I'm not fond of mice."

Susan put her face closer to the cage. "This one looks clean and healthy. Anyway, I like mice."

"I Googled it," said the middle-sized person. "It's a deer mouse."

"Well, we don't have to leave for a few more hours," said the deep-voiced human. "We can decide what to do with it then. The house we're considering is only a short drive around the forest, but we will have to go since I made an

appointment. Mean-
while, Susan, if you do keep
the mouse, even for an hour or two, you'll
have to take care of it. Feed it. Give it water."

"What do deer mice eat?"

"Famously, cheese."

"Do we have any left?"

"Think so."

"Is it a boy or a girl mouse?"

"No idea."

"Well, I think it's a girl. Can I take her out of the trap?"

"Ah . . . I'm not so sure that's a good idea. Not if you want to keep her. She's likely to run away."

"Why?"

"Animals don't like to be in cages. They want to be free."

"Then why did she go into it?" asked Susan.

"Perhaps she didn't mean to," said the middle-sized human. "She could have been fooled. It *is* a trap. Or, maybe she was hungry for the cheese."

"Sweetheart, I suggest you let her go. Remember, we're renting this place. The people who own it would not appreciate our bringing mice inside. That's probably why they put the trap out."

"But I want to keep her. I'm going to name her, too. From now on her name is . . . Spaghetti. My favorite food."

"That's a nice name."

Poppy, meanwhile, turned from one person to the next, trying, without success, to make sense of what they were saying. She began to think that she was not in any immediate danger. But since she couldn't be sure, she stayed in a corner, watched, and listened.

The girl stepped away from the table and left the room, only to come back soon with something orange in her hand. She broke it up into little pieces and squeezed them through the holes in the trap.

Food, thought Poppy, and her stomach growled. Not only did the orange stuff look good, it smelled good, too. All the same, she wasn't sure she should eat any. It was coming from humans. She found everything about them scary.

The larger humans smiled, and then went off.

"Enjoy Spaghetti," one of them called. "We're going to keep putting the picnic things in the car."

They left the room. Poppy had no idea where they went.

As for Susan, she rested her chin on her arms and continued to stare at Poppy. "I like you, Spaghetti," she said. Then she whispered, "I don't care what they say. I'm going to keep you."

Poppy, wishing she knew what the girl was saying, could only stare back.

— CHAPTER 18 —

Basil's Bunch

An impatient Ragweed had to wait a while before Basil returned. *He better hurry,* Ragweed kept thinking. *I don't like it here.*

When Basil did come he brought along eleven mice, male and female. To Ragweed's eyes, they seemed young and scruffy, not, at first glance, a bold team.

"Line up," commanded Basil.

The mice slouched forward and formed a ragged row. None were capable of standing still, but constantly shifted their feet and scratched their faces, bellies, and knees, pulled at whiskers, twitched tails, all the while stealing shy, hesitant looks at Ragweed. It was clear that they were not sure they wanted to be there.

"This," said Basil to the row of mice, "is Ragweed. Comes from the other side of the forest. A golden mouse, in case you wanted to know. The thing is, he found Poppy and was kind enough to let us know. As I told you, somehow she got herself caught in a human trap out past the creek. Down along Long Meadow, if I understand it. Ragweed here is willing to take us to where she is so we can get her free.

"Ragweed, this is Daisy, Trefoil, Candytuft, Glory,

Catchfly, Alyssum, Pansy, Zinnia, Primrose, Rocket, and at the end there, Toadflax."

"Hey, how's it going?" said Ragweed, wondering how he would ever be able to remember the names, though "Toadflax" stuck in his mind.

The eleven mice stared at him quizzically.

"Can you tell them," Basil said to Ragweed, "what we need to do about Poppy?"

"Okay," began Ragweed. "It's like Basil said, Poppy is caught in a trap. A human trap. It's all metal and closed at both ends. Tight as a turnip. She and I tried to get her out. Couldn't do it. You know, needs more jaws and paws. Thing is, we need to get her free—from out of there—before the humans who set the trap do something horrid to her."

"Are they the same humans who have been coming around here?" one of the mice asked Basil. "There's a rumor going around they might be moving in."

"Don't know."

"What kind of . . . of . . . nasty things do you think the humans would do to Poppy?" another mouse asked Ragweed. He thought it might be Zinnia. There had been a tremble in her voice.

"Anything from a total topping to nothing," said

Ragweed. "The point is, she's waiting out there for us to free her."

"And where," coached Basil, "is she?"

"Okay, sure. First, we'll have to cross your orchard"—Ragweed pointed—"and that little creek, and then go along what I guess you call Long Meadow."

"We're not going into Dimwood Forest, are we?" asked Catchfly in a timid voice.

Ragweed shook his head. "Only across the meadow. But there might be raccoons, snakes, and porcupines."

The eyes of the mice became big.

"Whoa . . . ," whispered one of the mice, his face suddenly pale. "Raccoons and snakes," he repeated, then rubbed his nose after which he squeezed his front paws tightly together.

"And did you say . . . *porcupines*?" asked another mouse in a shocked voice.

"I did see one," said Ragweed. "But that was in the forest, and I promise, we're not going there."

There was a tense silence and Ragweed thought he heard some hard swallowing. Tails visibly swished. A few mice looked at Basil, as if asking for reassurance.

"Was it a . . . a *big* porcupine?" someone finally asked.

"Not sure," Ragweed replied. "He was up in a tree."

One of the mice said, "Basil, did Lungwort give permission for us to go and do this?"

As Basil shook his head he said, "Be better not to tell him. So if you want to back out, this is the time to do it. But if we're going to save Poppy, as Ragweed said, we need to act quickly."

There was silence as each mouse decided whether to go or not. Sure enough, one of the mice suddenly looked up and said, "Sorry, Basil, I don't think I'll go. When I woke up this morning, I wasn't feeling well. Still don't." He stepped out of the line and ran back into the house.

The remaining ten mice shuffled their feet.

"Anyone else?" asked Basil.

The mice eyed one another uneasily. Tails quivered and there was some clearing of throats and a few ear twitches, although nothing more was said. Nor did anyone else leave.

"Okay," said Basil to Ragweed. "Let's go."

"Follow me," said Ragweed. With that, he bounded off the steps and headed for the old orchard. While he took the lead, the other mice formed a long, ragtag line with Basil at the far back to make sure no one else dropped out.

As Ragweed went forward, he glanced back at the mice. *This,* he thought, *is one rotten rescue team.*

CHAPTER 19

Across the Creek

THE LINE OF mice scampered by the pump, crossed through the old orchard, and continued on until they reached the banks of Glitter Creek. To Ragweed's eyes, the creek seemed no different than it had been before. Flowing steadily, it was making endless, frothy splashes and gurgles as the clear water tumbled against the mottled, moss-covered rocks. *Pretty,* thought Ragweed. But when the other eleven mice caught up to him they stood on the bank and regarded the water with faces full of unease.

One of the mice—Toadflax—said, "I've never gone farther than this. You guys?" The last was addressed to no one in particular.

"Nope."

"Not me."

"I haven't."

"I don't think *anyone* has. Except, I guess, Poppy."

"And now we have to rescue her."

One of the mice—Ragweed thought it was Catchfly—said, "Basil, we don't have Lungwort's permission to do this, right?"

"Nope," said Basil.

"You even ask?" questioned the one named Daisy.

Basil shook his head.

"Lungwort is *not* going to be happy," said Catchfly. "Is he?"

"Fact," someone else said, "he'll have a fit."

"And what's going to happen if we meet that porcupine that Ragweed saw?" asked another.

"And what about those raccoons?"

"And . . . snakes?"

Basil looked at Ragweed but didn't answer. That brought on more shifting of feet, ear scratching, and tail trembling, but no one else spoke.

All of a sudden, one of the mice—her whiskers were long and she was small—announced, "Sorry, guys. I'm not going across." She had been studying the water intently while slowly scratching her chin.

Ragweed had no idea what her name was.

"It's . . . it's too risky," explained the mouse without looking at anyone, all the while staring at the creek. She seemed to be waiting for a response. When none came, she shifted around, mumbled, "Have a nice day," and headed back toward Gray House. She went slowly, scratching an ear, head bowed, as if embarrassed.

Ragweed made a mental count of how many were left. Including him and Basil, there were only eleven of them.

Basil gave him a questioning look.

"We should be okay," said Ragweed. "But, hey, this is it. You either cross the creek or don't. We're going to need everyone."

"Right," echoed Basil.

No one budged.

"Okay," said Basil, "Ragweed is going to show us how to cross the creek."

Even as Ragweed asked himself why he always had to show the way, he tried to remember the route he had taken—over the rocks—to get across. After a quick study, he mentally mapped out a path to the other side. "Watch how I go," he called.

With that, he leaped onto the nearest rock and with something like a hop, jump, and a few more skips—covering fifteen stones in all—he reached the far side.

Cool, he told himself. *I'm good.* He turned and looked back across the creek. Not one mouse had followed him. Instead, they were all staring at the water, looking uneasy.

"See, guys, no problem," called Ragweed. "Now let's move it."

The mice on the other side continued to gaze at the fast-flowing creek, their tails jerking about. One mouse dipped her paw into the water as if to judge the depth.

"It's kind of cold," she said and shook her paw free of droplets as if they were unpleasant.

"Come on," Ragweed yelled. "You need to do it."

"Please, guys," said Basil, trying to encourage them to move forward. He was standing behind the other mice. "We're doing this for Poppy."

One by one the mice began to make their way across, using, for the most part, the same stones Ragweed had used, though moving with greater timidity, often hesitating between leaps.

They were almost all across when one of the mice—Ragweed thought it was Rocket—slipped and tumbled into the water.

There was a gasp from all the other mice.

Rocket, instantly panicky while trying to keep himself from being washed downstream, thrashed about and waved for help. Fortunately, Primrose was on a nearby rock. She reached down to the squealing mouse, grabbed one of his paws, and helped him clamber to safety—sputtering and spitting—onto her rock.

The two mice, much slower than before and tightly clutching each other's paws, jumped their way to the far shore. Once there, Rocket, dripping wet—which made him look like a wet, skinny noodle—shook his whole body to dry himself, soaking the other mice who were near.

Then Basil crossed over, trying to act as if he wasn't concerned.

That meant everyone was across save Trefoil. He remained on the far side, eyes fixed on the water, tail whipping about in great agitation.

"Come on, pal," called Ragweed. "Hit the hops."

"I apologize, Basil," Trefoil finally called out. "I don't think . . . I don't think I can do it."

"Sure you can," said Basil. "We did."

"No, I can't," cried Trefoil tearfully.

"Either you do or you don't," shouted Ragweed. "We have to haul."

After another long, silent moment, Trefoil shook his head. "Nope," he blurted out. "It's too scary." With that, he turned about and raced back in the direction of Gray

House, going much faster than he had come.

"Ten," said Ragweed as much to Basil as to himself.

"Let's get over to Long Meadow," urged Basil. "Away from the creek."

"And the forest," added Daisy, with glances at the other mice.

With Ragweed in the lead, the ten mice walked along the edge of the creek, until the meadow spread out on their right. Within moments they were all gathered under a meadow bush. Once there, Ragweed paused and tried to remember which way he had come. Along the forest edge, that was as much as he knew. "That direction," he said and moved accordingly.

The other mice followed in an untidy line, Basil as before, at the rear. The way they walked sluggishly from bush to bush let Ragweed know that not only had they never been in the meadow before, they also didn't want to be there now. All the same, he pushed on without pausing, fearful that if he halted even for a moment, others would go back.

Better hurry, he told himself, *before any more mice drop out.* So he even walked a little faster, calling over his shoulder, "Let's move it" in as brave a voice as he could muster.

But all the while he was thinking: *Hope I remember where Poppy is. Hope she's still there.*

CHAPTER 20

Poppy in the Log House

Inside the log house, deep within the trap, Poppy continued to watch the girl, even as the girl, her chin on the table, watched her.

"I'm so glad I caught you," said Susan. "I promise, I'll take good care of you. I will. Feed you and pet you. Keep your cage clean. Everything."

The middle-sized human came back into the room. "Honey, maybe keeping that mouse on the table isn't such a good idea. We eat there."

"But I want to watch her," said the girl.

"Why not put her over here," said the human. "You can sit on the couch and still see her."

"Oh, okay." Susan picked up the trap—with Poppy inside—and set it down on a much smaller, lower table.

Then the girl sat back on the couch and continued to keep her eyes on Poppy.

The other human left the room.

Poppy stared back at the girl. Only then did she realize something: *That Ragweed, if he did go to Gray House, and if he did get my family to come and try to rescue me, since I've been moved, they won't be able to find me. I'll never get free.*

Poppy made a decision: *If I'm ever going to get out of here, I'll have to do it myself.*

Susan squirmed forward on the couch to be a little nearer to Poppy. "I don't care that Daddy thinks mice are dirty," she confided in a whisper. "Or that he doesn't like them. You know what, Spaghetti? I'm going to keep you forever and ever and ever."

CHAPTER 21

The Mice in the Clearing

Ragweed peered out from beneath the cover of the bush where he had paused. Before him lay a low, open, grassy area. Under the bright, warm sunlight, he became fairly certain it was the same clearing in which he had helped that snake wiggle out of its skin.

Good, he thought. *That means we aren't far from that log house—and Poppy.*

"We're close," he called back as his jittery band of mice struggled to catch up with him.

"Might give them a bit of rest," whispered Basil, giving a backward nod. "They aren't used to this sort of hike. Me neither."

"Sure," agreed Ragweed. "While we do, how about going over everybody's name again so I can remember them."

"Okay, guys," called Basil. "Line up for a name check."

The eight mice arranged themselves in an untidy line. There was considerable twitching and shifting while apprehensive eyes kept looking all around, to their friends as well as to Ragweed.

Basil stood behind them. "This is Daisy," he said, putting a paw atop one of the mice heads. Daisy was small and dainty, with big, staring eyes that had long, dark lashes.

Basil moved to the next. "Glory." Glory was stocky with big ears, a short nose, and stubby whiskers.

"Candytuft." She was small, with big staring eyes, and front paws that kept squeezing each other.

"Catchfly." Skinny, Catchfly had deep pink eyes and small paws. She kept staring intently at Ragweed as if not believing what she was seeing.

"Zinnia." The largest of the mice, Zinnia had a long tail that kept lashing about as if much agitated. When she darted furtive looks at Ragweed, she kept blinking her eyes. The light seemed too strong for her.

"Primrose." Primrose was a plump mouse, with small, stumpy, and slightly bowed legs, but the look on her face was fierce. While standing there she kept her front paws clenched.

"Rocket." Still damp, Rocket was sitting up on his rear

legs, constantly rolling his front paws one over the other, while his eyes kept gazing around at the bushes as if he had never seen anything so unusual.

"And Toadflax." Toadflax was the smallest of the mice, but he had a long tuft of fur on his head, dyed blue, which kept falling over his face. He was constantly brushing it back, with sudden swipes of his front paws. His jaw was clenched.

Ragweed gazed at the eight mice and couldn't help but think: *they sure aren't the most fearless-looking creatures.* Then he reminded himself that though they had never traveled so far from Gray House they had, more or less, managed.

Zinnia, the largest mouse, raised a paw.

"Yes?" said Basil.

"Basil, I'm sorry. I'm afraid I'm not going to be able to do this. And I just remembered that my mother asked me to do something, which I never did. I . . . I think it would be better if I went home."

Before Basil could respond, Zinnia turned about and raced away in the direction they had come.

Catchfly turned to watch her go. Ragweed wondered if she, too, would leave. The rest of the mice grew twitchier than before. But no one said anything until Basil said, "Sorry," to Ragweed.

"Nine of us," he said.

"Will that work?" asked Daisy.

"It's what we have," replied Ragweed with a shrug. But he was thinking, *I hope so.*

"How about telling us what we're going to do?" asked Toadflax as he pushed the fur tuft out of his eyes.

"Sure," began Ragweed, "here's the deal. Not too far from this place, Poppy is in that trap. Least she was last time I saw her. It's like a cage. The trap has closed doors at both ends. And—the trap is sitting right next to a human house.

"Poppy and I tried to open the trap. Couldn't budge it. I'm hoping, you know, that all of us—together—can lift one of those end flaps."

"How are we going to do that?" asked Catchfly.

Ragweed, not wanting to admit he had no real plan, only said, "You'll learn when we get closer."

It was Candytuft, her blue eyes large, who said, "Ah, Mr. Ragweed, sir . . . are . . . are those humans . . . around there?"

"Maybe."

Toadflax said, "And what happens if we can't open the trap?"

"Not good," admitted Ragweed.

"And . . . and what'll we do if . . . if those . . . humans appear?" stammered Rocket. He pulled hard on his nose.

"Not sure about that either," said Ragweed.

The look on Primrose's face turned angry. "Well," she demanded, "what *are* you sure about?"

Ragweed said, "Only that if we don't get Poppy out she might be totally snuffed."

No one said anything to that. There was complete silence.

"Guys," said Basil after a moment. "We have to try. For Poppy's sake."

The tense mice fidgeted but said no more.

"Okay, then?" said Ragweed. "Everyone ready? The house—and the trap—are not too far beyond this grassy spot. Nothing between us and Poppy. Let's hit it." That said, Ragweed stepped forward onto the grassy area. The other mice started to follow. It was at that moment a cry came from out among the trees:

"Ragweed!"

At that instant, Ragweed stopped moving, as did all the other mice.

"Who's that?" whispered Glory in a frightened voice.

"Ragweed!" came the cry a second time.

"Who's calling you?" demanded Toadflax.

Ragweed, knowing exactly who it was, muttered, "Dang!"

CHAPTER 22

Lotar Again

LOTAR RUSHED OUT onto the grassy area.

"Back off," cried Ragweed.

The mice—seeing the young raccoon—needed no warning but scrambled back to the protective branches of the bushes at the edge of the clearing. Once there they crouched down and kept their eyes fixed on the raccoon.

For his part, Ragweed dashed to a tall bush, crept up behind its leaves, and then peeked out to see what the young raccoon was doing.

Lotar, standing on his hind legs in the middle of the grassy area, was gazing around. "Ragweed," he called. "Where are you?

Please come back. We can have a playdate."

Ragweed, not wanting Lotar to discover him or the other mice, remained motionless, fairly sure the big mama raccoon would soon appear. Sure enough, within moments, she did, moving slowly into the clearing toward Lotar.

"Lotar," she called out in a weary voice. "We've searched enough for your friend. We have to stop. I'm afraid he's gone."

"That's because you threw him away," returned the young raccoon. "How would you like it if I threw a friend of yours away?"

"I'm truly sorry I did," said the mother raccoon. "I didn't understand everything that happened. I'm truly glad your friend helped you and brought you home. But Lotar, what's done is done. All this chasing around for that mouse has to stop. I'm exhausted. We need to go back to the cave where we can both take a nap."

"I don't want to nap."

"If you don't, I do."

"Can't I spend a few more minutes looking for my best friend?" pleaded Lotar. "Can't I? Please."

"A few more moments. That's all." The big raccoon lay down in the middle of the grassy area. "Goodness," she said. "It's warm."

"Ragweed," Lotar shouted. "I'm right here. Please come.

My mama is sorry she threw you away. Aren't you, Mama? Say it."

The mother raccoon already had her eyes closed.

"Mama," called Lotar. "You have to say you're sorry you threw Ragweed away. Loudly, so he can hear you. Or he'll never come back."

The young raccoon went up to his mother. "Mama? Are you asleep?" He gave his mother a soft poke. After a moment he said, "I guess so."

Lotar stood up on his hind legs and looked around the clearing again. Then he began to wander around. He had not gone more than a few feet when he suddenly stopped. "Oh my gosh," he screeched. "Mama. Look. I think it's a snake."

Ragweed, from behind the bush leaves, had been watching and hearing it all. *Dude,* he thought, *it's a snakeskin.* He would have called out but had absolutely no desire to let Lotar know he was so near.

"Mama," whispered Lotar. "There's a snake here in the grass. I'm scared. Wake up, please. You need to get it away."

Ragweed waited. Surely, he thought, the mother raccoon was going to wake up. But the exhausted raccoon remained sleeping.

Lotar began to run away from the open place, far from the snakeskin, and deeper into the meadow.

"Bummer," said Ragweed. "He's going right toward where Poppy is."

From behind Ragweed an impatient Basil softly called, "Ragweed, what's happening?"

"Dude, chill a bit."

At that moment, the mother sat up. "Lotar?" she called. "Lotar! Oh, baby, where did you go now? I'm so tired of all this running around. You must come back—now!"

Lotar, however, was gone.

Ragweed watched as the mother raccoon came to her

feet, gazed around the clearing, and then began to walk away, looking and calling for Lotar, her long tail twitching with annoyance. But she went in a direction altogether different than Lotar had taken, not even noticing the snakeskin.

Ragweed listened as the fading voice kept calling, "Lotar, baby. Where are you? You must come back . . . now."

Then silence.

"All clear?" asked Basil.

"All clear," said Ragweed.

The mice crept into the clearing.

"Were those animals . . . raccoons?" asked Glory, her big ears twitching.

"Yup," said Ragweed.

"We've been told to avoid them," said Catchfly. "They might harm us."

Primrose turned to Ragweed. "How come that one was calling your name?"

"Yeah, do you know him?" asked Glory.

"Little bit."

"I don't think we want anything to do with raccoons," said Daisy, her eyes bigger than ever.

"Don't worry," said Ragweed. "No one is going to hurt you."

He looked out over the clearing, which was now completely clear of the raccoons. As far as he was concerned, there was nothing to keep him and the mice from going straight to the trap to rescue Poppy. Then he realized something: Lotar was now *between* where he and the mice were, and where Poppy was. And these mice were scared of raccoons. That meant that unless he could find a way to get that raccoon baby out of the way, he would never be able to reach Poppy.

CHAPTER 23

Poppy

WITHIN THE LOG house, Susan remained sitting on the couch, her eyes steadfast on Poppy. The Havahart trap—with Poppy inside—was on the low table.

As for Poppy, she was crouched in a far corner of the trap, all the while peering anxiously out at the girl. *This is bad,* she told herself. *Worse than before. There's absolutely no point in waiting for that Ragweed. He'll never find me in here. I need to do something on my own.*

The girl continued to chat away, telling Poppy everything about her life, her parents, what she did in school, the books she liked to read, the things her family enjoyed doing during their vacation, and the new house they—that day—were going to decide if they would buy.

"But my mommy and daddy will have to fix it up because a lot of the house is broken," she explained. "They call it a handyman's special. But if we move there I'm not sure where I'll go to school. I hope I'll like it. I'll have to make new friends. But you," Susan said, "will be my first new friend in my new house."

As the talk went on, Poppy found she was unable to resist the smell of the cheese that the girl had put into the trap. Cautiously—as Susan continued to chatter—Poppy crept forward and ate all the cheese.

Susan leaned forward. "Did you like eating that?" she said. "Would you like some more? Mommy said I have to feed you." She wiggled off the couch. "I never did eat all my breakfast. I'll be right back and give you some," she called to Poppy. "Don't go away."

CHAPTER 24

Ragweed Has an Idea

In the grassy clearing, Ragweed tried to decide what to do. He knew he had to hurry because his mice companions were extremely nervous—more so since seeing the raccoons—and he knew they were all too likely to give up and bolt back to Gray House without rescuing Poppy.

But between where he, the mice, and that house (with the trap) stood, was Lotar, that annoying young raccoon. Ragweed was sure his mice companions would not go anywhere near that animal. He didn't want to either. That meant he would have to find a way to chase Lotar away. As for the humans, all he could do was hope they did not come back.

While Ragweed tried to figure out what to do, his eyes fell on the discarded snakeskin. Seeing it reminded him that Lotar had been so frightened by it he had run away. That gave Ragweed his idea.

"Dudes," he called back to the mice. "The raccoons are gone. We're completely safe."

With extreme caution, the mice crept out from the protection of the bushes.

It was Basil who said: "Ragweed: that raccoon who was here, he knew your name. He's not a friend of yours, is he?"

"Nothing but a nuisance," replied Ragweed. "Besides, I've figured out a way to make sure we'll never see him again."

He went up to the snakeskin and gave it a poke. It was as light as a leaf.

"Dudes," he called to the mice. "Come on over here."

The mice approached timidly. Seeing the skin, Candytuft halted and gasped: "What *is* that thing?"

"Used to be a snake," Ragweed assured her while giving the skin another jab. "It's nothing alive. A cast-off skin. But I have an idea how we can use it."

"How?" asked Rocket, who was staring at the thin skin with a mix of fright and fascination.

"Okay," began Ragweed, "that young raccoon is between us and Poppy, right? The thing is, you saw it, he's afraid of snakes. Totally. Here's the deal. We'll all get under this empty skin, and, like, walk along, pretending to be a live snake. I promise, if that silly animal sees us, he'll run away."

"How are we going to do that?" asked Glory. As she asked, she exchanged doubtful glances with the other mice, her own short whiskers quivering. "It's a tube."

Ragweed bent over, gingerly picked up the tube of snakeskin, and with his sharp front teeth sliced the skin open from one end to the other. "Okay," he said, spitting out a bit of snakeskin. "Come on. Basil, your help, please. We need to do this. Everyone line up alongside the skin. I'll stay up front, so I can, you know, lead the way. Basil, stay to the rear and keep everyone moving."

With a great deal of caution, the mice stood in a line alongside the snakeskin.

"Now," said Ragweed, "I'll give a count of three. At three, hoist the skin up and bring it over your heads, and then—when I give the word—lower it."

"How will we move?" asked Daisy.

"Hold the skin up with your forepaws, and keep your rear feet on the ground," explained Ragweed. "Since I'll be up front, you can all follow me. I'll be leading. Get it? We'll look like a snake, but we won't be. Make sure to keep yourself inside the skin so the raccoon doesn't see you. We'll be heading toward Poppy. You cool with this? Okay, grab hold of the skin. Ready, one, two, three . . . lift."

As one, the mice, with only a few puffs and grunts, lifted the split skin.

"Now, hoist it over your heads," Ragweed cried.

The mice did as told.

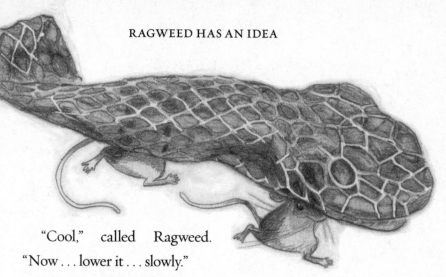

"Cool," called Ragweed.

"Now . . . lower it . . . slowly."

The mice did that, too.

Ragweed, who had stayed free to watch what happened, was pleased. The long snakeskin was off the ground, the mice were halfway inside the skin, though their feet could be seen. It looked like a centipede.

Satisfied, Ragweed dived under the skin's front part and held it high enough with his front paws so he could see where to go.

"Totally cool," he called back. "Okay, dudes, ready to move? Poppy, here we come. Mice, march! One, two, three . . . Hit it."

With that, Ragweed began to move. The other mice followed him. It was as if a snake was traveling forward.

Now, thought Ragweed as he peered ahead, *I bet I don't have to worry about that silly raccoon.*

CHAPTER 25

What Lotar Did

W HEN LOTAR FLED from the snakeskin, he had hurried away from the clearing. As he went, he constantly glanced over his shoulder wanting to make sure he was not being followed.

"Hate snakes," he kept jabbering. "Really, really, really hate them. Hate, hate, hate. Snakes. They have sharp teeth. So sharp. Which bite. Mama warned me. She hates them, too. 'Keep away from snakes,' she said. 'And people and dogs. That's what she said and that's what I'm doing.'" He rushed on. "Keep away. I am. I am."

Feeling more secure the farther he went— and with no snake in sight—the young raccoon began to slow down until he finally stopped and peered back. "Good," he said. "No snakes. I got away. I'm a good runner. I am."

Tired, Lotar sat down and gazed around at the surrounding meadow only to realize that he recognized none of it. Though he kept looking around, it didn't take long before he grasped that he had no idea where he was.

"Mama?" he called.

No answer.

"Mama? I think you lost me again."

He remained still for a few moments. Then he shouted, "Ragweed-mouse. Guess what? I lost my mama again. I need you to come back and find her. And me, too. Can you hear me?"

No answer.

Lotar considered going back to where he had been—the clearing. But there, he knew, was where that snake had been and he wanted to be as far away from that terrible creature as he could.

After waiting some more, the young raccoon got up and moved in the direction he had been going, ambling slowly through the meadow bushes and grasses. Now and again he paused and called, "Mama. Where are you?" And then: "Ragweed. You need to come and find me."

No one answered. All Lotar could see was tall grass,

RAGWEED AND POPPY

shrubberies, plus here and there some flowers. *Where am I?* he kept asking himself. *I wish someone would find me.*

He had moved on a little farther when he was surprised to see an open space in the meadow ahead. Cheered, he went forward a more few paces, then stopped and peeped out from behind some bushes. What he saw was a huge pile of logs, one stacked upon another. At one end of the pile was a tall, rectangular hole.

It was the log house.

To Lotar, who had never seen anything like it before, it appeared to be some kind of cave, but unlike his rock home, one made of wood. *Does anyone,* he wondered, *live inside it?*

To add to his puzzlement, standing right next to this pile of wood was a large box, all shiny blue. It had round things attached to its side. Also, on the side of the box that Lotar was facing was a hole.

Even that was not the most surprising.

Two creatures—the likes of which Lotar had never seen before—were putting some things into the back of this shiny blue box.

Then Lotar remembered what Ragweed had told him about people. He gasped. "They look like those people— with fur on their heads—which Mama said to keep away from."

150

From the edge of the meadow, the young raccoon stared at the humans with fascination. He was now sure he understood what they were, but never having seen any before, he wondered what they *did*. What were they putting into the big blue box?—a basket and some smaller things? Lotar's biggest concern however was, could these people hurt him?

The young raccoon decided it would be safer to study these people creatures for a while and see what they did. Sitting back, he waited and looked on.

CHAPTER 26

Poppy in the Trap

FROM WITHIN THE trap, Poppy watched Susan leave the room. Feeling better and stronger because of the cheese she had eaten, she examined the room with new energy. What she observed was a table, some chairs, a couch, plus a fireplace along with a nearby pile of cut wood. Most importantly, Poppy saw that the window and door of the house were open. She decided that if she could get out of the trap, she'd be able to bolt away and get free of the house.

Using two paws, she worked hard to pry open the bars of the trap. But as before, her efforts proved useless. Nonetheless, she also struggled to push open the flaps at each end of the trap. That, too, proved as impossible as before. Discouraged, she sat back. *It's stupid,* she scolded herself, *to keep doing the same useless things. I have to try something new.*

Susan came back into the room. She was holding food in her hand.

"I've got it for you," she said. "From my breakfast." She held it out so Poppy could see it.

For a horrible moment, Poppy thought the girl was holding the body of a mouse. Narrow and gray brown, it was some three inches long, the color of her own fur. After sniffing, Poppy realized, to her great relief, it really was some kind of food.

The girl sat down on the couch. "It's a sausage," she said. She leaned forward and pushed the sausage against the trap holes only to giggle. "That's stupid of me," she said to Poppy. "It's much too big. How am I going to get it into you?"

As for Poppy, the mere thought—though wrong—that the girl was holding a mouse completely took away her appetite. She retreated into the farthest corner of the trap, hunkered down, and watched the girl.

Susan, in turn, studied the trap. After a moment, she set the sausage down and tried to open the end flaps. She could not do it.

"I'll get Mom or Dad to open it," she said and bounded up, saying over her shoulder, "Be right back."

Poppy, watching the girl go, tried to figure out what was

happening. Perhaps, she thought, it had something to do with the food and opening the trap. *If the girl opens one of the trapdoors,* Poppy told herself, *that might be the best—and only— moment to get free.*

Susan returned. "They're packing the car," she said. "After we look at that house we're going on our picnic. I'll ask if you can come." She sat on the couch again and continued to study the trap.

"You know what?" she said. "I better shut the doors and windows in case you get out. I don't want you to run away, ever."

Poppy watched with disappointment as Susan shut the windows and front door. Then the girl came back and continued to study the trap intently.

"Oh," the girl suddenly cried. "I see how it works now. There's a hook that keeps that trapdoor shut. I bet I can open it. Then I can feed you."

Susan knelt down in front of the low table and put both hands around the trap.

Poppy watched her every movement.

Using one hand, the girl managed to flip over the bar hook that kept the trapdoor locked. Then, with her other hand, she wedged her fingers under the trapdoor and lifted. Both of her hands were fully engaged.

It also meant—Poppy suddenly realized—that in that moment the trap was open.

At that instant, she shot forward, racing as fast as she had ever run in her life, out through the open end of the trap. Once free, she raced across the table. When she reached the table's edge, she gathered all her strength and leaped.

The girl screamed.

CHAPTER 27

What Lotar
Also Did

As Lotar sat in the meadow, gazing at the blue box and the strange people, he heard the girl's scream and realized it came from within the pile of logs. Whatever it was that the people were doing by the big blue thing, they instantly dropped everything—even leaving a hole in the blue box—and ran into the log house.

Delighted that the people had gone, Lotar waddled out from under the bushes. Cautiously, he approached the shiny blue box. What, he wondered, was it for? He was also curious to know what those creatures had been putting inside it.

He drew close to the box's side and stood up on his hind legs but was not tall enough to look in through the open window. Even as he tried to see inside, he heard a noise behind him. Startled, he glanced back over his shoulder. To his absolute horror, a gigantic snake was coming out from the bushes. The snake was coming directly toward him.

Terribly frightened, Lotar hardly knew which way to go. The big blue box was right in front of him, blocking his way. But that hole was there. He looked back. The snake was still coming. It was his fright that gave Lotar extra strength. Using all of it, he leaped up and forward, only to tumble down inside the box, landing on a seat. Still panicky, the raccoon pulled himself up and looked out the hole through which he had fallen. The snake was still coming.

Lotar searched for an escape. He turned. In front of him it looked like nothing, but when he reached forward to touch it with his claws, the space turned out to be hard. *Good,* he thought, *that snake can't come at me that way.*

Turning, he saw a big wheel sticking up, and near to it, a bunch of buttons. Since they looked interesting, Lotar scurried over, stuck out a claw, and touched one of the buttons. When he did, all kind of different-colored lights flashed on. There was even a loud roar and the blue box shook. Delighted, Lotar touched the buttons again. The roar stopped. The lights went out, followed by a few loud clicks. Lotar had no idea what it all meant.

Wanting to see the lights again, he pushed yet another button. That time a piece of that hard see-through stuff began to rise. The hole through which he had come into the box closed up.

Puzzled, Lotar studied the clear, hard thing for a moment. He even went over to it but when he poked it a few times with his claws, he realized that though he could see through it, it was solid. The snake would not be able to get in. *That was good. But, how did that hole close up? Was it something I did? If it's hard, how come I can see through it?*

There were, he now realized, more holes in this shiny thing. The trouble was, all of them now had that solid stuff in them.

But, he told himself, that means there's no way that snake can get to where I am. *I'm safe. Really safe.*

Except that was also the moment when Lotar realized something else: yes, the snake was outside, and he was safe inside, but he had no idea how he would be able to get out. What if those large people returned?

I know, Lotar told himself. *I'll hide. Maybe after a while the holes will open again and that snake will be gone.*

With that, Lotar wiggled off the front seat, and to his delight found a dark, empty space under it. He crawled deep within and after making himself as comfortable as he could, curled in a ball and shut his eyes tight. Closed eyes meant he could see no danger, which was a good thing. In moments he was asleep.

CHAPTER 28

Ragweed

RAGWEED, FROM HIS position up front under the snakeskin, watched Lotar standing beside the blue car. Then he saw the raccoon notice the snake and become frantic. It was what Ragweed hoped would happen. But what Ragweed did not expect was that the young raccoon—clearly frightened—would leap straight up and disappear *into* the car.

Whoa, thought Ragweed. *That raccoon is double-down dumb.*

"Halt," he called. The eight other mice under the snakeskin stopped, bumping into one another.

"What is it?"

"Why did we stop?"

"Is something the matter?"

"Is that raccoon there?"

"It's hot under here."

Ragweed kept his eyes on the car, hoping Lotar would reappear. He did not.

"Ragweed?" called Basil from the far end of the snakeskin. "What's happening?"

"Not sure," said Ragweed, standing still. He had his eyes on the car and was watching when a sudden loud roar came from it. But the sound ceased as quickly as it began. Glass rose up in the same window through which Lotar had gone.

What, Ragweed wondered, *is that dumb raccoon doing?*

Ragweed waited. Nothing else happened.

"Can't we get out from under this thing?" called Candytuft, who was in the middle of the skin. "It's hard to breathe."

"Follow me," called Ragweed. Instead of going forward, he led the mice around in a circle and headed back under the protection of some bushes. "We can rest here," he said. "Throw the skin off."

The mice lifted the snakeskin and put it to one side.

"That was hard work," said Toadflax, pushing the blue fur out of his eyes.

"Did anything bad happen?" whispered Daisy.

Basil approached Ragweed. "Did that raccoon go away?"

"Not exactly. Did you see that blue thing? The car?"

"Sure."

"That raccoon went in it."

"What he's doing there?"

"Hiding, probably."

"Are we safe?"

"Think so."

"But," asked Basil, "where's Poppy?"

"She must still be in the trap."

"Where's the trap?"

"On the other side of the car. Behind that house."

"What do we do now?"

"Give me a minute," said Ragweed. "I'll think of something."

CHAPTER 29

What Happens
to Poppy

EVEN AS POPPY leaped off the table, Susan continued to scream, "She got out! Spaghetti got out!"

Poppy landed squarely on the wooden floor. Seeing only one safe place to go, she tore under the couch. Though the space was dark and dusty, she didn't care. She was free of the trap.

Jubilant, she scampered as far under the couch as she could go, until a wall blocked her from going farther. Once there, panting from her efforts, she looked back from where she had come.

Susan's face—eyes streaming tears—was pressed right against the gap between the couch and floor.

"Spaghetti," she called. "Please come back." She reached her hand as deep under the couch as she could, fingers wiggling, trying to get hold of Poppy.

Seeing what the girl was trying to do, Poppy pressed herself tighter against the wall.

Susan's hand wasn't even close.

"What's happened?" Poppy heard a voice call. "Why are you screaming?" It was one of the other humans.

"Spaghetti got away."

"Oh my. How did that happen?"

"I was trying to feed her a sausage, but when I opened the cage, she ran out."

"A sausage? Oh, honey. Where'd she go?"

"Under the couch. I think."

"This is what I was afraid of. Bringing mice into a house that's not ours. I didn't think it was a good idea."

"I didn't mean to," said Susan, tears streaming down her face. "Please help me get her."

When Poppy saw more human faces peer under the couch, she worked to shrink herself down even smaller.

One of the humans said, "I see her. She's pushing herself against the wall."

"Can you grab her?"

To her dread, Poppy watched as a large hand reached under the couch. As the wiggling fingers came closer, Poppy squeezed even harder against the wall, so tightly she found it difficult to breathe.

The grasping hand pulled back. "I can't reach her," said a voice. "She's under too far." The hand withdrew.

"Would a broom help?"

"Good idea. And a flashlight—if you can find one—so I can see her better."

Susan's voice: "Hurry. She'll get away."

Poppy saw Susan's tearful face again, peering under the couch. Simultaneously, she heard the sound of footsteps moving out of the room.

"Sweetheart, Daddy's gone to fetch a broom."

Susan's face vanished.

Poppy peered out. None of the humans were looking at her. No one was reaching for her. Knowing she must get farther away, she scurried along the wall until she came up against a big wooden post at the end of the couch. She peeked out but saw no humans. What she did see—not too far away—was that jumble of wood pieces she had noticed before. The sticks were stacked haphazardly, leaving many gaps. After a quick study, Poppy was sure that if she could reach the pile, she'd be able to creep in among the sticks and logs and hide safely.

After double-checking to make absolutely certain that none of the humans were between her and the wood, Poppy shot out from under the couch and ran, tail straight behind her, and dived headfirst among the pile of wood.

She heard nothing from the humans.

Poppy squirmed as far among the logs as she could go. The wood that surrounded her smelled sweet. The darkness was soothing.

Poppy paused to let her heart stop pounding. *You did it,* she told herself, elated by her success. *You freed yourself.*

Then she reminded herself: *but you are not yet out of the house.*

She listened intently. Within moments she heard the sound of the humans returning to the room.

"Each of you go to an end of the couch," said a voice. "I'll find her and poke with the broom and try to force her to run out. The two of you need to be at either end to catch her. Susan, shine the flashlight under the couch."

Poppy crept through the woodpile until she could peek out into the room. What she saw was the biggest of the humans lying flat on the floor before the couch. In one hand, he held a long stick. As for the little human, she was crouched down at one end of the couch—the end from which Poppy had escaped—holding something that had a bright, shiny light. The other human—the middle-sized one—was at the other end of the couch.

Poppy, amidst the wood, watched and waited.

After a few moments, the deep-voiced human said, "I'm sorry. She's gone."

"Gone? What do you mean?" said one of the other humans.

"I can't see her."

"Where," said an unhappy Susan, "do you think she went?"

"No idea."

"Did she disappear?" said the girl. She was miserable.

"Looks that way."

"But I want Spaghetti."

"Honey, I'm afraid Spaghetti wants her freedom."

"But I want her." The girl began to sob.

"I'm sorry, sweetheart; she's vanished. Maybe there's a hole in the floor under the couch. By now she could be under the house. Or even inside the couch. Anywhere. Mice like holes."

"It's probably just as well," said the deep-voiced person. "I keep telling you, it's not healthy to have a mouse in here. And it's not our place."

For a few moments, no one spoke.

"I have an idea," said Susan as she suppressed her tears.

"What?" said one of the others.

"I'll put the trap back where it was."

"Why would you do that?"

"That mouse went into it once. Maybe she'll go back in again."

"Honey, do you think she'd do that?"

"I want her to."

"You might want that, but I don't think she would."

"She might."

"Well . . . Is this the food you were trying to feed her?"

"Uh-huh. The sausage. It almost looks like her."

"Okay, sweetheart, you can try, but I don't think she'll go in again. My guess is that she's learned her lesson not to go into a trap."

"I want to try."

"If you want to do it, sure. Put the sausage deep into the trap and then place it back outside in the same place where it was."

"Okay."

"But . . . I need to warn you, that mouse will probably not go back in."

"I want to see if she does."

From her hiding place in the woodpile, Poppy watched one of the humans pick up the trap. The middle-sized human opened one of the flap ends, placed the sausage bit into the far back of the cage, then locked one flap open with the side rods.

The trap set, the three people marched out of the house, leaving the door open behind them. Poppy saw them turn to the left and continue on.

She was alone.

Breathless, wanting to be absolutely sure the people had left the room, Poppy waited a few more moments. When she was certain the people had walked out of the house, she squirmed from the woodpile onto the floor. Once again, she looked all around. Convinced that the people had left,

Poppy galloped across the floor, over the threshold, and out the door.

Since she had seen the people turn to the left, she went to the right.

Poppy was completely free.

CHAPTER 30

How Ragweed
Rescued Poppy

STANDING AMONG LOW bushes at the edge of the meadow, Ragweed kept his eyes fixed on the blue car. When nothing else happened, when Lotar did not reappear, he turned to Basil.

"Cool. Looks like that dippy raccoon is going to stay in that car."

"What about Poppy?" asked Basil.

"Right," said Ragweed. "Like, we need to get over to the trap and check in with her. At least we can tell her, you know, we're here. Should cheer her up. Then we'll figure out what we have to do to get her out. You good with that?"

"Sure."

"Let's go."

When Basil informed the other mice what he and

Ragweed were doing, the seven mice were happy to sit down near the snakeskin and rest under a bush.

Leaving them, Ragweed and Basil crept out from the protection of the grasses. Even as they did they saw three humans appear. The smallest one was holding something in her hands.

Ragweed and Basil halted immediately, squatted down, and watched what the people were doing.

Ragweed groaned. "Bummer," he said to Basil. "Those people have the trap."

"The one Poppy is in?"

"Looks that way." Ragweed stared. The people had been moving fast, but Ragweed was sure he had seen *something* in the trap that certainly appeared almost the same color and size as Poppy, curled up in a corner. "Yup," said Ragweed, "she's still in there."

"Why are they moving her?"

"No idea."

The two mice watched as the humans marched around to the back of the log house. Then they saw the smallest of the three people—the one who was holding the trap—bend over and place the trap in almost the exact spot it had been before.

When the trap had been put down, one of the humans said, "Now, Susan, you have to be patient and leave it alone. If she does come back—which I doubt—it will take a while."

Ragweed and Basil continued to watch as the three humans returned to the house.

All was quiet. Nothing moved.

"Have any idea," whispered Basil, "what they are trying to do with Poppy?"

Ragweed shook his head.

After some more intense watching, Ragweed turned to Basil and said, "The big thing is, she's still in the trap. I'm sure she is. And it looks like the people are going to leave her alone."

"Is she . . . is she still alive?"

"Sure hope so."

For a moment, the two mice continued to stare.

"What are we supposed to do?" asked Basil.

"Since she's still in there," said Ragweed, "it doesn't change anything. Like, I need to get over and talk to her. Make sure she's all right. Least I can do is, you know, tell her we're here. Might make her feel better. But, with all these people around, maybe it'll be safer if I go alone. You head on back and stay with the others. Keep them calm. And out of sight. Another thing: be ready to put the snake-skin back on in case either of those raccoons comes back. Can you handle all that?"

"Think so," said Basil, and he scurried back to where the other mice were waiting.

Left alone, Ragweed studied the scene. There was still no movement from the car. He was sure Lotar was still inside it.

Good. Stay there.

As for the humans, he had seen them go back into the house and not come out.

Good there, too.

Ragweed turned back toward the trap. Nothing had moved. *Total nothing,* Ragweed told himself. *No one to bother me. People or raccoons. Which means I'm safe. Which also means I need to move. You've taken enough time. Go rescue Poppy.*

He took a few steps toward the trap, paused, peered around again, but saw nothing to alarm him. *There is absolutely no danger,* he scolded himself.

He took a deep breath, tensed his legs muscles, said, "Go," and dashed forward.

But as Ragweed approached the trap, he slowed down and then stopped. He stared hard. *Was* she in there? There was absolutely *something* or *someone* tucked into the far corner of that trap, precisely at the place where he had told Poppy to hide.

"Cool," he said. "It's got to be her. Good thing I'm here to save her."

But then . . . once again Ragweed hesitated. He sniffed. Something did not smell right. He looked again. *Like, how come, you know, she's not moving? Is that her?* The more he stared the less sure he was. *But it has to be Poppy,* he told himself.

"Hey, Poppy girl!" he called. "You asleep?"

No response.

What's going on? Maybe shutting her eyes isn't her only trick. Shutting her ears might be, too.

He inched closer.

"Poppy!" he called again, louder. "It's me, Ragweed. Back from Gray House. With your cousin Basil. With a whole bunch of your family. Hey, I'm about to get you free."

When there was still no reply, Ragweed inched closer to the trap. Then he realized that one end of the trap was open.

Wait a minute. How did that happen?

He decided it didn't matter *how* it happened. The important thing was that the trap was open. Which meant Poppy could get out. If she noticed. *If she was awake.*

"Poppy," Ragweed called in an even louder voice. "Wake up. The trapdoor is open. You can get free."

He saw no movement.

Ragweed kept staring. *Does Poppy,* he thought, *even know the trap is open? Maybe she managed to lift that end and was so exhausted by the effort she fainted.*

Or maybe she is asleep. Which means she isn't too smart. After all, Ragweed reminded himself, *she did tell me she had wandered into the trap with her eyes closed. Maybe I have to tell her the trap is open.*

He looked back. He could see Basil watching him from within the grasses. He was surrounded by all of the other mice, peeking out and gazing at him intently.

Ragweed had to smile. He loved the notion that they all were watching him. *I'll show them what a mouse can do,* he thought. *Right. A mouse has to do what a mouse has to do. Cool. I'll be a hero. Here I go.*

He gave his friends a casual wave as if he wasn't excited. Then he edged forward until he was facing the open end of the trap.

"Poppy!" he yelled as loud as he dared.

No reply.

Do it, Ragweed said to himself. *Show everybody how brave you are. Time to save Poppy.* For a second, he paused to touch his dangling bead earring and was reassured that it was there.

All good, he told himself. *Go!*

With that, Ragweed shot forward, plunging headlong into the trap, aiming right where he was sure Poppy lay asleep. He was so eager to reach her, he didn't look where he was going. Halfway in, he tripped on a plate of metal, banging a knee.

Next instant, there was an enormous *crashing* sound as the trapdoor came down behind him. It shook the whole cage. Ragweed, intent on reaching Poppy, paid no mind but rushed on. Only when he reached her—or what he had thought was her—did he realize it was *not* Poppy.

Bummer. It's not her. Some dumb food. Something's wrong. A bolt of panic shot through him. *Yo, dude. Get out of here.*

Whirling around, Ragweed tore back toward the entryway, only to come to a fast halt. He stood there, stunned, staring, trying to grasp the situation: the flap was shut.

Which meant that he was caught in the trap.

"Dude." Ragweed sighed. "You are in trouble."

— CHAPTER 31 —

Poppy

WHEN POPPY RUSHED out of the log house, it took but a few seconds for her to turn the corner and plunge into tall, protective grass. There, trembling with relief, she paused. "I'm out," she cried. "Out. And I did it all by myself." Elated with her triumph, she stood in place, heart fluttering. Taking a deep breath, she allowed herself to feel the bliss of freedom.

Oh, I'm so proud of myself, she thought and was aware that she blushed with pride, even as, at the same time, she couldn't help but giggle. "I did it," she said yet again. Then, because it felt so good to say, she said it again: "I did it."

Thoughts of home filled her head. *Oh my,* she told herself, *I so want to get back to Gray House. How wonderful it will be to get there. And if I can tell that nice mouse—the one named Ragweed—that*

I freed myself, it will be so good. It'll save him a trip back and he might even think a little better of silly me, dancing into that trap with my . . . No, she scolded herself, *do not go dancing again.*

With a joyful shake of her whole body—even as she firmly resisted the urge to dance—Poppy took a step forward only to hear:

"Help. Will someone help me? Please."

It was not merely the cry that stopped Poppy: it was the oddness of the words. What she was hearing was so much like what she had called out when *she* had been caught in that awful trap. It was as if she was having a bad dream, a memory about a nightmare that had already happened.

"Help," the call came again. "Will someone come and help me. Please."

Unsettled—and considering the possibility that she had lost her mind—Poppy moved cautiously forward until she reached the end of the log house. Once there, she crept on a little farther, paused, and peeked around the corner.

She was surprised to see the trap. Only then did she remember watching the girl carry the trap out of the house. Not that she had known what the people were intending to do with it. Now it appeared as if the girl had set the trap back down precisely where it had been before, on that patch of short grass near the flowers.

Humph. Did that girl think I would go into it again? I may be silly but I'm not stupid.

Poppy's impulse was to run off in the opposite direction as fast as she could and have nothing to do with that trap or the people. She was about to do exactly that when the cry came again:

"Hey! Isn't there anyone to hear me? I want out."

That held Poppy: the voice was familiar although she could not place it. She took a few more steps toward the trap only to realize that someone was in it, back to her.

She stared. It was another mouse. Altogether astonished, she drew closer. That was when the mouse in the trap turned around and Poppy saw who it was.

"Ragweed!" she cried.

Ragweed clutched the trap bars with his two front paws. "Dude, am I glad to see you."

"But . . . but," Poppy stammered, "what are you doing in there?"

"Like," returned Ragweed, "what are you doing out there?"

"I got free on my own."

"Hey, did you forget you asked me to rescue you? I thought you were sleeping in here. So when I hurried inside, I hit the switch, you know, or whatever it is. I couldn't get out. I'm stuck in here."

"Stuck?" asked Poppy, hardly believing what she was hearing and seeing.

"Don't you remember," said Ragweed, "we tried everything to get you out. Right? Same thing. The bars won't give and the trapdoors are shut—tight. So here I am."

"But . . . but what about Gray House?" said Poppy. "Did you ever go there?"

"You serious, Dude? I went the way you asked me." Ragweed went on to tell her about Basil and the other mice.

"Is Basil *near*?" asked Poppy, still finding it hard to believe what she was hearing—and seeing.

"Sure. Right over there—that direction, in the meadow," said Ragweed. "Go on over and you'll see for yourself. I need you and your family pals to drum over here in double time and peel me out. With enough paws, you know, we should be able to lift the flaps. That was our plan, remember?"

Poppy stared over at the meadow. She was finding it hard to believe what had happened; she outside the trap, Ragweed inside, members of her family close. She saw no sign of Basil or the other mice. "Are you sure they're near?" she asked.

"You disbelieving me? Absolutely. I brought them here. To free you. The way you told me. I'm telling you"—Ragweed pointed—"they're right over there. You need to bring them over here fast. I want out."

"Okay. I'll get them. Be right back." With that, Poppy started to run.

"But hurry," she heard Ragweed call after her. "I don't want to stay here forever."

As Poppy ran around the corner of the house, the first thing she saw was the blue car. That made her stop. But when she realized it was not moving, and that none of the people were near it, she continued on toward the meadow. She had covered half the distance when an enormous animal stepped out of the meadow grass. The animal, with an angry look on her face, was calling: "Lotar. Where are you? Can you hear me? Come back. Lotar."

As soon as Poppy saw the animal she turned and raced off in a completely different direction—her back to the animal, the car, Ragweed, and Basil—telling herself, *You need to hide.*

CHAPTER 32

Lotar and His Mother

"LOTAR!" CRIED THE mother raccoon. "Where are you? Can you hear me? Come back!"

Lotar, asleep inside the car, heard his mother and woke up. It took him a moment to recall where he was; under the blue car's front seat, where he had been hiding.

"Lotar! Where are you? Answer me."

"I'm right here," Lotar replied. Then he realized his mother probably would not be able to see or hear where he was. He worked his back onto the seat.

"Lotar!"

Standing on his hind legs, the young raccoon looked out through the car's side window. Quite plainly, he saw his mother on the road below.

"Here I am," he called.

His mother heard his voice, but when she looked around she could not find him.

Lotar banged against the door with his claws. "Here, Mama. Here."

The mother raccoon looked up and saw Lotar at the car window. "What are you doing in there?"

"I ran away from a snake."

"What snake?"

"The one that was chasing me. The biggest snake in the world. It doesn't like me. And you told me they bite."

"Where did it go?"

"I don't know."

"I'm glad you ran from that snake," said the mother raccoon. "But you need to come out of there this instant."

"I can't."

"Why?"

Lotar banged on the glass again. "This box won't let me out."

"How did you get in?"

"This stuff"—Lotar poked at the glass window again—"wasn't there."

"Are you sure?"

"No, I'm not sure. But, Mama, guess what? There are these big animals around. The only fur they have is on their heads. Ragweed told me they are people."

"We need to keep away from them, too," said the mama raccoon.

"Will they hurt me?"

"They might."

"What should I do?"

"Can you hide some more?"

"I was under a seat."

"Then get right back under it, fast. Stay there and keep quiet. I'll try and figure out what to do."

"Okay." With that, Lotar climbed over to the back seat and crawled under it. "This is a safer space," he said. "More room." He settled down to wait.

Outside, his mother stared at the blue car and tried to think what she might do to get her baby free.

CHAPTER 33

Susan and the Mouse

Inside the log house, a sad Susan sat on the couch while her parents stood before her. "Do you truly think," she asked, "that my mouse won't go back into the trap?"

"Honestly, honey, it's not likely. But by the time we come back from looking at that house, I suppose it might happen."

"Why do we have to go?"

"Because I called and made an appointment to meet with the real estate agent and go over the house. He did say he'd bring his dog. You like dogs."

"I like mice better."

"And some construction workers will be there, too. If we are going to buy that house and live in it, there's a whole lot of repairs we'll need to do. Most of all we have to see if we can afford it."

"It's a stupid house," said the girl. "I don't like it."

"I don't know if it's stupid. It *is* run-down."

"We simply have to fix it up," said the middle-sized person.

"I hate it," said the girl. "It's old. And ugly."

"I'll admit, the farmer who owned it did not take good care of it."

"What happened to the farmer?"

"We don't know."

"What was his name?"

"Lamout. Farmer Lamout."

"I don't like him either."

"Honey, it's only because the house is in such poor shape that we might be able to afford it. Anyway, there's a lovely old orchard and a nearby creek. Maybe we'll be able to fish in it. Or we could dam the creek up and make a swimming hole. Wouldn't that be fun?"

"I told you, I don't want to live there. I like where we live."

"We understand. It can be hard to move. And we probably won't. But for the moment, we promised to go over there and meet those folks. So please, don't fuss, and come along. It's only a short drive, a few miles away. Maybe you can play with that dog. And I've packed a picnic for after we look at the house."

"Okay."

All three—the mother, father, and the girl—went out of the house and walked toward the car.

"Look," cried the girl. "What's that?"

It was the mother raccoon sitting at the edge of the meadow.

"Where?"

"Right there."

Startled by the sight of the people, the raccoon turned and ran back among the meadow bushes.

"It's gone," said the middle-sized person.

"What was it?" asked Susan.

"Not sure," said the tallest human. "Some kind of wild animal. It ran away too fast for me to tell."

"Why was it sitting here?"

"No idea."

"Did it go after my trap?"

"I doubt it."

"But maybe," said Susan, "my mouse went into the trap and that animal grabbed it."

"Sweetheart, I seriously doubt your mouse went back into the trap. But if it makes you feel better, go run and check. Just do it quickly. We need to go. Those people are expecting us."

The girl ran behind the log house. As soon as she saw the

trap, she stopped and stared. Inside the trap was a mouse.

"Spaghetti," cried the girl. "You came back. You did."

She rushed to the trap and picked it up with her two hands. Running, she raced back to the car, holding the trap high.

* * *

A dejected Ragweed had been sitting in the trap, wishing Poppy and Basil would hurry, when the trap was suddenly snatched up by a human and lifted away. Taken by surprise, Ragweed had no idea what was happening other than he was being carried somewhere.

* * *

"Spaghetti came back," cried Susan as she ran to the car with the trap in her hands. "Spaghetti came back."

Her parents gathered around and stared into the trap.

"That's certainly amazing."

"Must be a stupid mouse."

"Spaghetti is *not* stupid," said the girl. "She came back because she loves me. She wants to move into our new house and live with us."

"Honey, I don't think I'd like that. How about putting it down and getting into the car. We need to go. We'll be back soon, and that mouse won't be going anywhere."

"I want to take her with me."

"I'm not so sure . . ."

"So she can see our new house."

"Honey, we—"

"I'll keep the trap on my lap. I won't open it."

"Okay. Fine. But sweetheart, please, we're late. We have to go."

"And don't open that trap. I absolutely don't want that mouse in our car."

"I promise."

The three got into the car. Susan sat in the back seat with the trap on her lap.

With a roar, the car's motor came to life.

As she settled into her seat Susan picked up the trap and looked closely at Ragweed. "Guess what?" she said. "Spaghetti changed her fur."

"Honey, I doubt that."

"She did. I'm sure she did. It's a different color. It's sort of golden."

"Well, if you say so."

"It's true."

"And she's all dressed up. With an earring."

"You do have a good imagination."

The car swung around and started down the dirt road.

* * *

Under the rear car seat, Lotar dared not move. All that noise and shaking. *What's happening?* he asked himself. Then he reminded himself what his mama told him: *Stay where you are and keep quiet.* So that's what he did.

* * *

Inside the trap, Ragweed heard the sound of the car motor and sensed the car was moving. He looked up at the girl who was smiling down at him.

This is crazy, he told himself. *I'm being hauled away and I have no idea where.*

* * *

From within a tall clump of meadow grass, the mother raccoon watched with dismay as the blue car began to move down the road.

"They're taking my boy away," she cried and began to race along, following the car. Abruptly, she stopped. She remembered that the road circled around the Long Meadow. *I'll cut through and catch up with it on the far side.*

With that, she rushed off in an easterly direction.

CHAPTER 34

What Poppy Did

Poppy, having run away from the large animal, hid among some thick weeds. Once there, she crouched down, listening intently, hoping she had not been seen. Hearing the sound of human voices, she stayed low. Within moments there was a loud roar—which she remembered as the sound of the car. With great care, she parted the weeds and peeked out in time to see the blue car move down the dirt road and disappear.

"Good," she said. "I want nothing more to do with them."

Even as she saw the car move off in one direction she also saw the large animal bound off in the opposite direction.

Good again, Poppy thought. *Everybody's gone. That'll make it easier to free Ragweed.*

Feeling safe, Poppy moved from her hiding place and went to the edge of the meadow. "Basil," she called out. "It's me, Poppy. Ragweed said you were here. Basil, are you close?"

Basil, a look of amazement on his face, stepped out of some weeds. "Poppy? Is that you?"

"Of course it's me. Who else would I be?"

"But . . . that mouse—that golden mouse—that Ragweed—he said you were caught in a trap."

Poppy, unable to keep from grinning, said, "I freed myself."

"How'd you manage that? I mean, Ragweed told us it was impossible for you to get out by yourself, that he needed a whole bunch of us to do it. Which is why we're here. Hey, guys," he called. "Come on out. It's Poppy. She's free."

One by one, Daisy, Candytuft, Glory, Catchfly, Primrose, Rocket, and Toadflax came out into the open.

"Hello, everyone," called Poppy. "Thanks for coming."

"Hey, Poppy," said Toadflax. "We thought you were in a trap. But I guess you're not." It was hard to say if he was pleased or disappointed.

"Yeah," said Catchfly. "We came all the way through Long Meadow to free you."

"I was able to free myself," said Poppy. "But now it's Ragweed who's in the trap."

"Ragweed?" cried Basil.

"Is he in the same trap you were in?" asked Primrose.

Poppy nodded.

"How'd he do that?" said Daisy.

"Not sure," answered Poppy. "But we need to hurry and get him out before the people come back. They just left."

"Are you positive they went away?" asked Basil.

"Absolutely. I saw them," said Poppy. "Come on. Let's go help Ragweed."

Primrose hesitated. "Wait," she said. "Wasn't there also a raccoon around?"

"What's a raccoon?" asked Poppy.

Basil described them.

"I did see one of those. A big one. But it ran off," Poppy

told them. "Not sure where, but it's gone. Come on. We have to get Ragweed out. It's awful being in that trap."

She turned and headed back toward the far side of the log house. The other mice, following, trooped along.

Basil went along by her side. "Was it Ragweed who got you to come?" Poppy asked him.

"He did. He's an interesting mouse. But I don't think Lungwort was nice to him."

"Did Lungwort say it would be all right for all of you to come and try to rescue me?"

Basil shook his head. "We never told him."

Poppy paused. "Will you get into trouble?"

"Maybe."

"Sorry. But I appreciate your coming."

"Wasn't easy. But it doesn't seem as if you needed our help. How'd you do it?"

"I'll tell you later. We need to free Ragweed."

With Poppy in the lead, the mice turned the corner of the log house. Poppy stopped and stared, not sure she had come to the right place.

"What are we supposed to be looking for?" asked Rocket as the other mice joined Poppy and Basil.

"The trap," said Poppy, hardly believing what she was not seeing. "It's . . . it's gone."

"What's gone?"

"I told you. The trap."

"You sure we came to the right place?" asked Basil.

A baffled Poppy continued to gaze all around. "I'm mostly sure."

"Then what happened to that golden mouse?" said Primrose.

"Yeah," said Daisy. "Where's Ragweed?"

"Or the trap?" added Toadflax.

"I don't know," said Poppy, thoroughly perplexed. She went where she was sure the trap had been. "Look," she said. "The grass is all matted down here. The trap was here. It was."

"But . . . how could it move?"

"Don't know."

"Poppy," said Basil, "are you absolutely certain that Ragweed was in it?"

The other mice looked at Poppy doubtfully.

"I'm . . . mostly sure," said Poppy, though she had no explanations.

"He must have gotten out on his own and left," said Basil. "When he and I first spoke at Gray House, he told me that as soon as you were free he would move on."

Poppy, trying to make sense of it all, said, "I guess that's what happened. He saw I was free and then got out on his own. He did seem smart. Wish I could ask him how he did it."

No one said anything until Toadflax asked, "What do we do now?"

"Yeah," said Daisy. "I guess we did what we came to do. Got Poppy free."

"I suggest," said Basil, "we go back to Gray House. If we move fast enough we might even get back without Lungwort noticing we were gone."

"Good idea," said Poppy as she continued to stare at the spot where the trap had been. Then, wondering if she would ever see Ragweed again and feeling a deep disappointment that she probably never would, she turned and headed for Long Meadow. The other mice followed.

CHAPTER 35

At Gray House

A BATTERED GREEN PICKUP truck came along the Tar Road and halted in front of Gray House, backfired once, twice, released a smelly cloud of fumes, and then shuddered as its motor stopped rumbling. On the side door of the truck was a sign:

THE DERRIDA DECONSTRUCTION CO.
AMPERVILLE

Seated in the cab was a large man with gray hair and a wrinkled face. He wore a green baseball cap with the word "AMPS" on it. Though the truck was no longer moving, the man continued to sit in his truck, hands on the steering wheel, gazing at Gray House, as if appraising it.

On the seat next to the older man sat a red-faced young fellow. His cap had the letters "SF" on it in orange.

"That's it," the older man said to the younger. "The old Lamout place. Used to be nice. Real wreck now, isn't it? If it was up to me I'd knock it down."

"Be easy with a bulldozer," offered the young man.

"A cinch," agreed the older man. "But some city people say they're interested in buying and saving it. I'm not so sure they know what they're doing. Be a lot of work. Expensive. The roof is no good. You can see that for yourself. Anyway, I need to check the foundations and basement before they show up. Oh well. Come on. Those folks should be here soon. And there's a real estate guy coming, too."

*　*　*

Old Plum was standing on the front porch when the truck arrived. He took one look at it and cried out, "The humans are back. The humans are back. Everyone hide."

At once, the mob of mice that had been milling about in the front yard and on the porch talking, playing, or resting, erupted into panic. They took up Plum's cry, "The humans are back! The humans are back!"

Tails high, tails low—whiskers stiff with tension—pushing, shoving, and scrambling—with a chaos of

squeaking, squealing, and moaning, plus shouts of, "Out
of my way," "Faster," Move it," "Get off my foot"—the
mice flooded up and over the lopsided porch and poured
through the open doorway and into Gray House.

Once inside, outdoor mice were joined by indoor mice,
who were also caught up in fright.

"The humans are back!"

Some raced down the steps to the basement. A large
number sought safety in the many closets. Others streaked
up the stairs to the attic.

Plum ran, too, but he headed for Lungwort's old boot. Once there, he yanked aside the striped curtain and yelled, "Lungwort! The humans are back! Did you hear me? Lungwort. Humans coming. You better get out!"

Sweet Cecily emerged from the boot. She looked blankly at Plum, made her nervous gesture of flicking one of her ears, and asked, "What did you say?"

"The humans are back," cried a breathless Plum. He pointed toward the main doorway.

"Where?"

"Out front. Two of them. In a truck."

"Are they the ones who were here before?"

"Don't know. But I think they're going to come into the house."

"Oh dear," said Sweet Cecily. "I'd better tell Lungwort." With that, she retreated into the boot.

Plum waited anxiously, his tail swishing about in great agitation, all the while constantly shifting his worried eyes to the front doorway.

Lungwort emerged from the boot, eyes blinking in the light, paws adjusting his thimble cap on his head. It remained lopsided.

Sweet Cecily stood behind Lungwort, looking over his shoulder.

Lungwort cleared his throat and stroked his whiskers. "All right, Plum, is there some little difficulty that's disturbing you?"

Plum pointed toward the doorway. "The humans are back," he said again. "Two of them. In a car, or a truck. Whatever it is."

"What are they doing?"

"Not sure. Sitting there. Looking at the house. I think they're about to come in."

Lungwort drew himself up. "All right then, you need to get everyone to assemble," he said. "I'll give a speech so I can tell them what to do."

"What will you say?"

"Have no fear. I'll think of something."

Plum turned and ran off, shouting, "Meeting! Meeting for everyone! Lungwort is going to tell us what to do."

Lungwort turned to Sweet Cecily. "Do I look distinguished?" he inquired.

She considered him. "You might want to curl your left whiskers a bit more."

"Ah, yes," said Lungwort, and he did just that. Then he proceeded to march over to the old straw hat and climbed up (with an assist from Sweet Cecily from his bottom) until he reached the crown.

Once on top, he tapped his head thimble to set it at the proper angle, gave his whiskers another slight curl—with additional attention to the left whiskers—coughed loudly to clear his throat, and then looked around. He was expecting to see the entire mice family—all two hundred and fifty—gathered before him, giving him, Lungwort, their full attention, waiting for his speech. But there were absolutely no mice in sight, other than Plum who was standing below, looking up, even as the skinny creature kept glancing anxiously toward the doorway.

"All right, Plum," said Lungwort. "Must I ask? Where is everyone?"

"I think . . . I think they're hiding," said Plum.

"Why?"

"Because . . . I told you . . . the humans . . . are coming—"

"But I didn't give permission for them to hide."

"Lungwort," said Plum, "they're afraid." He stole another peek toward the doorway. "Because . . . the humans."

"If there is something of which to be afraid," said Lungwort, "I shall tell them. And provide good advice. They always need to be told what to do."

"Yes, Lungwort. I understand. I do. I'll find some . . ." Plum ran off.

"Lungwort," called Sweet Cecily from the bottom of the hat, "don't you think we better hide, too?"

"Well, I don't know . . . speech first . . . action second. The family needs me to instruct them. After all, I'm the head of this—"

Plum returned, shooing seven scared mice before him. "Hurry," he said to them. "Lungwort is going to speak. You need to listen so you know what to do."

"But . . ."

"Never mind," said Plum. "Stand right here. Show respect. Look up. Pay close attention. Lungwort," he called up. "These are all I could find."

The few mice, plus Plum, stared up at Lungwort who was perched high above them on the straw hat. The attention of the agitated mice, however, was divided, because they kept looking past Lungwort toward the front door.

Lungwort, having finally gathered an audience, drew himself up, tapped his thimble hat, and began: "My dear family. We are gathered here at a difficult moment. It has been rumored—merely rumored—that some humans are approaching our happy home. Fortunately, I am here to tell you what action to take. It seems to me that you need to—"

There were the sounds of heavy footsteps on the front porch. Then a rapping sound came, which was followed by a booming human voice that shouted, "Anybody home?"

At that, the seven mice who had been listening to Lungwort bolted away in seven different directions. Plum ran off, too, heading for one of the closets.

Even Sweet Cecily went her own way, racing into a different closet.

Lungwort, alone, remained standing upon the old hat, frozen. "Fortunately," he repeated, "I am here to—"

A human voice called out, "We're coming in."

Lungwort looked behind him toward the doorway and saw a large, moving shadow—human-shaped—advance. With a jolt of fright, he leaped off the hat, raced to the old boot, and plunged inside, pausing only to make sure he drew the necktie curtain shut behind him.

When the man with the green hat walked into the house there was not one mouse to be seen.

CHAPTER 36

Poppy Leads the Way

IT WAS BASIL who led Poppy back along Long Meadow. They had not gone far when Poppy suddenly halted and gasped. "What's that?" she cried, pointing to the snakeskin. It was lying on the ground.

"Old snakeskin," said Toadflax, proud of himself. "We used it to chase away a raccoon."

"The raccoon I saw?" said Poppy.

"Could have been," said Primrose.

"It worked, too," added Daisy. "Soon as he saw the snakeskin, he ran away."

"One of Ragweed's ideas," said Basil. He explained what they did.

"The raccoon I saw was big," said Poppy. "And it looked angry."

"The one we chased was small," said Primrose.

"What happened to it?" Daisy asked Poppy.

"Told you. Ran off."

"Is it still around?"

"Don't know," admitted Poppy. "Could be. Do you think we might meet it again?" Poppy asked Basil.

"It's possible. I'm guessing these raccoons live around here."

"Maybe," suggested Toadflax, "since we're going back to Gray House, it would be a good idea to use the skin—the way we did before—in case we see those raccoons again—either one."

"You guys good with that?" Basil asked the other mice.

"That's smart," said Toadflax.

With everyone eager to get back home, no one objected.

"Okay," called Basil, "back in line."

Basil turned to Poppy. "It was Ragweed who led us here. Think you can guide us back to Gray House?"

"Hope so," said Poppy, trying hard to remember her dance through the meadow.

"Then get up to the front of the skin," said Basil. "You can see best from there."

"Sure."

The mice quickly aligned themselves along the snakeskin with Poppy at the front.

Basil gave the commands. "Ready, lift," he called. Up

went the skin. "Get under." The mice—along with Poppy—stepped beneath the skin. "Lower it." Down came the skin.

Poppy, at the head of the skin, peeked out. She could see well. "Everyone ready?" she called.

There was a chorus of "Yes," "Sure," "I'm good."

"Then—let's go," Poppy called, and the mice began to walk forward so that once again it appeared as if a snake was moving along.

Going slowly, the mice traveled through Long Meadow with Poppy choosing the route, following the way she best remembered. Though the skin was not heavy, moving along on their hind legs, front paws held high, was exhausting for the mice.

"No pushing."

"Slow down."

"You're stepping on my feet."

Now and again, Poppy paused to let everyone rest.

"How close are we?"

"We'll be at Glitter Creek soon," Poppy said by way of encouragement.

They continued on until, hearing the sound of the rushing water, she said, "Almost there."

They soon reached the banks of the creek. Thrilled to be so near home, and looking for the best place to cross over, Poppy continued to lead the way along the banks.

They were about to reach the crossing when she suddenly called out, "Stop!"

"What is it?"

"Something wrong?"

"What's happening?"

"Shhh," said Poppy. "No talking."

Right in front of them, on the banks of Glitter Creek, Poppy had caught sight of the mama raccoon.

The other mice crept out from under the snakeskin and watched in silence. The large raccoon was gazing at the rushing creek water as if knowing she would have to cross over, but uncertain how best to go forward.

"That one is a lot bigger than the one we saw," said Toadflax.

"Right," said Basil. "Much bigger."

"Scarier," said Primrose.

"Shhh," cautioned Poppy. She looked beyond the raccoon and saw Gray House in the distance. *Almost home,* she thought and felt a glow of excitement. A troubling notion came to her: *Is that raccoon going to Gray House? That would not be good. We need to get that animal to go somewhere else.*

It was Candytuft who said the obvious, "That raccoon is blocking our way."

"Is it going to Gray House?" asked Daisy.

"I think," suggested Toadflax, "we should use the

snakeskin to chase it away. Like we did the other time."

Basil studied the raccoon. "Good idea. If we scared it from here, most likely it'll run upstream. Once it goes, we'll be free to get across."

"That'll be good," agreed Primrose.

"Okay, let's try," said Poppy.

Basil gave the commands. "Up. Down." Once again, the mice were within the skin.

"This time," suggested Basil, "I think we should make some noise. Hiss, like a snake. That'll make sure the raccoon will hear us."

The mice began to hiss as loud as they could. "SSSSS."

"Go!" called Poppy.

The mice inside the skin with Poppy in the lead began to move.

* * *

The mother raccoon was still staring into the water when she heard the hissing mice. She looked back and saw what appeared to be a large snake coming right at her. Taken by surprise, and altogether alarmed, she leaped directly away, landing in the creek waters. Sputtering and thrashing, she was big enough to touch creek bottom. She splashed across. Once on the other side, thoroughly soaked, the raccoon looked back, saw the snake was still there, and began to run in the direction of Gray House.

"Oh dear," said Poppy, watching the raccoon rush across the creek and then keep running. "It's going in the worst possible direction. Gray House."

"What do we do now?" asked Daisy.

It was Basil who said, "That raccoon sure doesn't like snakes. If we can get the skin across, we can keep using it to make sure it doesn't go into Gray House."

"Not going to be easy," said Poppy.

The mice gathered at the water's edge.

"Let's get across," said Basil.

"I'll go first," said Toadflax.

The mice formed a line, and this time, while not inside the snakeskin, each one held an edge of it with a paw.

Toadflax took a leap. While he wobbled some, holding on to the skin steadied him and kept him from falling.

Poppy followed.

The other mice came, too, the skin both balancing and pulling them along, until they had reached the far side, the snakeskin intact.

"Good job," said Basil. "Back under the skin. Poppy, you might as well stay up front. Keep watch for the raccoon. If we see it, we'll try to keep it away from Gray House. Okay, here we go."

"Wait!" The call came from the other side of the creek. The mice in the snakeskin threw it off and looked back.

On the far side of the creek was Candytuft.

"What are you doing there?" cried Basil.

"I had . . . I had to go behind some bushes."

"Never mind," said Rocket. "Come across."

Candytuft curled her tail about her toes. "I . . . I don't think I can."

"You have to," said Poppy. "We need to get home fast."

The other mice gathered at the creek's edge and watched.

"It's not hard," called Daisy.

Candytuft came to the water's bank. She studied the rocks, made her front paws into fists, then jumped, one rock, two rocks, and a third rock. There she stopped. Eyes wide with fear, she looked about. "I'm scared," she said.

It was Toadflax who jumped back out over the creek rocks, got near Candytuft, and held out a paw. "Hold on."

Candytuft gripped the paw and, helped by Toadflax, the two went across the rocks until they reached the other side.

"Everybody okay?" said Basil.

"Yup."

"Back under the snakeskin."

Once again, the mice moved, but this time they were heading through the orchard directly toward Gray House.

Thank goodness, thought Poppy. *Almost home and everybody's safe.*

CHAPTER 37

At Gray House

A SMALL RED CAR pulled up in front of Gray House. Mr. Jack Sonderson, the real estate agent, unfolded himself from the front seat and stepped out onto the road. Tall and skinny, he was dressed in a pale blue suit, white shirt, and a striped tie.

Pausing briefly, he noticed the pickup truck, then stood before the house and momentarily appraised it. Finally, he turned back to his car. "Come on, Dudley."

A large brown dog with a sharp nose and floppy ears jumped out. "Good boy," said Mr. Sonderson, and he gave the excited dog a scratch behind one of his ears. The dog looked up and wagged his shaggy tail. After attaching a leash to Dudley's collar, the man said, "Don't think we'll be here too long."

With Dudley the dog—on the leash—trotting along at

his heels, Mr. Sonderson went up to Gray House and onto the front porch. The boards, he noticed, squeaked. He put a hand on the porch rail. It wobbled. Some of the rails were only attached at one end. *About to fall apart,* he thought. He went to the doorway and since there was no door, he leaned over the threshold and shouted, "Hello. Anyone here?"

"I am," returned a voice. The large man with gray hair and a green peaked cap—the man who had come in the pickup truck—stepped out through the doorway, onto the porch. His assistant, the young man, also came forward. The older man held out his hand to Mr. Sonderson.

"Todd Gruffin. Derrida Deconstruction Company. You the real estate guy?"

"Yes, sir. Jack Sonderson. Amperville Real Estate. Pleased to meet you." The two men shook hands.

Mr. Gruffin said, "Nice-looking dog. What kind is it?"

"Golden retriever. He's a good hunter. Goes after rats, squirrels, raccoons, foxes . . . anything."

Dudley suddenly lurched toward the open doorway, pulling on his leash. Mr. Sonderson had to hold him back with two hands.

"Steady, Dudley," he said, easing his dog back with the leash and a pat on his head.

Unable to move forward, the dog whined and barked loudly five times.

"Sit," said Mr. Sonderson to the dog. Dudley sat but whimpered with frustration, his tongue lolling.

"Looks like he smells something," said Mr. Gruffin with a grin. "Do you have people who want to buy this place?" he asked. "It's a wreck."

"Yes, sir," Mr. Sonderson answered. "They seem to think they can fix it up."

"Have they seen it?"

"A few times, I guess. Amperville folks. A couple with one kid. Gave me a call. So, yes, they're interested."

"I don't know," said Mr. Gruffin with a shake of his head. "I'd think it would make more sense to knock it down and start again."

"I'd love to do that," offered the young man.

"Well, the land is nice," said Mr. Sonderson. "And the price is low." He looked at his wristwatch. "They should be coming along any minute," he said. "I'd better step in and have a look around for myself."

Mr. Sonderson turned to his dog. "Dudley, you need to stay." He tied the dog's leash to a porch rail, said "Stay" to the dog again, and walked into the house. Mr. Gruffin followed along with the young man.

The dog sat, whimpered some, barked twice, but remained in place, panting.

Mr. Sonderson wandered around the front room,

staring at the floor and the ceiling. Sniffed. "You're right. Must have been mice here a while back," he said. "Lots of them. No wonder Dudley barked."

"Yeah, something," said Mr. Gruffin.

Mr. Sonderson picked up a boot that was on the floor. "The farmer's old shoe and necktie," he said and flipped both into a corner. "What a mess."

"Folks got too old to run the farm. Moved to the city." Mr. Gruffin kicked a straw hat and sent it skittering across the floor. "Must be old Lamout's straw hat," he said. "Want me to tell these people how bad the place is?"

"Sure," said Mr. Sonderson. "They need to know."

"Okay. But, I mean, it's in bad shape."

"But it does have possibilities," said Mr. Sonderson. "Lots of closets. And the house has a good setting. Quiet. It could be lovely. I'll walk around until those folks arrive."

* * *

Lotar's mother hurried across the orchard. When she reached the old pump, she paused and studied Gray House. She recognized it as a human house but saw nothing to deter her. In any case, she was much more interested in the road that passed in front of the house. Hopefully, that blue car—with Lotar inside—would be passing along soon. The

question was, would she be able to stop it? It was frightful to consider, but if she had to, she would stand in the middle of the road to bring it to a halt. No matter what, she was not going to let her boy be taken away.

She hurried on. Avoiding the house, she crossed the road and found a hiding place in a clump of wildflowers. Gray House was right across the way and she could keep watch on the road.

Satisfied she was in the right place, the big raccoon squatted down and waited for the blue car to appear.

★ ★ ★

Led by Poppy, who had remained at the front of the snakeskin, the mice moved through the orchard.

"See anything of that raccoon?" called Basil from the rear.

"Not so far," Poppy answered.

"Where'd it go?" asked Primrose.

"Hope it didn't go to Gray House," said Glory.

"Lungwort wouldn't like that," said Rocket, giggling.

"Hopefully, it went somewhere else," said Poppy and continued to lead the way toward Gray House. *It will be so good to get back home,* she thought. *What I need is some peace and quiet.*

CHAPTER 38

In the Blue Car

W HEN THE BLUE car left the log house it moved slowly down the dirt road. Susan's father was driving. Her mother was in the other front seat. Susan was in the back. Once she had settled into her seat, Susan pushed a button on the door handle. Her nearest window rolled down, letting in lots of fresh air. She bent over the trap. Ragweed was squatting in a corner of the trap, staring up.

"Is having the window open okay?" Susan asked him.

Not understanding, Ragweed simply looked back at her.

* * *

Lotar, out of sight under the back seat of the car, remained crouched in the dark space. He was trying to guess why the blue box was shaking and rumbling so. *It feels as if it's moving,* he told himself. *If it is, where am I going now? Do these people know I'm hiding beneath the seat? Mama said to keep away from people and stay quiet. But what are these people going to do with me? I hope Mama knows where I am so she can rescue me. But where is she?*

If I am moving, it's like being on that train. Good. Ragweed can come and help me find my mama the way he did before.

Lotar almost called out, but—thinking of the people—decided that he'd better keep quiet.

Ragweed sat in a far corner of the trap, which remained on the girl's lap. He continued to stare up at her, wondering what she was saying. By craning his neck, he could also see out the window and observe the rapidly moving landscape.

I'm going somewhere again, he realized. *Wonder where?* As he sat staring at the girl, it was impossible for him not to ask himself: *What's going to happen to me this time?* Maybe I'll go

back to the city. He turned.
The girl was looking at him
as if expecting him to say
something. He gazed back
and touched his earring. It
was safe. *Glad that something is.*

"How could this mouse change the color of its fur?" Susan
asked her parents.

"Are you sure it has changed?"

"Uh-huh."

"Sometimes shifting sunlight can make colors look different."

"No, it's different. It is."

"If you say so," said the girl's mother, but it didn't sound
as if she believed it.

Susan didn't care. She knew it was true and she loved
the fact. "I have a mouse who can change her fur," she said
with pride.

* * *

Ragweed, wishing he understood what the people were
saying, kept thinking: *Nothing to do but be patient again. It's*

boring being patient. Wonder where that Poppy went. Would have liked to have said goodbye to her. She was nice. Hey, you know, whatever happens, happens.

* * *

"How long will it take to get to that house?" asked Susan.

"Not long. We'll be off this dirt road soon. Then a regular road. Called the Tar Road. A few minutes."

"What are we going to do when we get there?"

"We'll look at the house again, and decide if we like it. We'll try to learn everything we need to do to fix it up. People to give us advice regarding repairs will be there, too. And the real estate guy."

"And," insisted Susan, "we can see if Spaghetti wants to live there."

"Susan," said her father sternly. "Let me say it again; I don't want *any* mice in the house. I'm going to be honest and say I'm not even happy to have one in the car."

"But I love mice," said the girl. She bent over the cage and said to Ragweed, "Don't worry. I love you."

"Susan, I'm sorry, you simply cannot take that mouse into the house. We can't allow that. If you wish, you're welcome to stay in the car with her. That's your choice. But, I have to say, it would nice if you looked at the house again. You might be living there."

"Oh, okay."

* * *

Crouched among the clump of flowers by the side of the road, the mother raccoon kept staring along the Tar Road. It was not long before her determination was rewarded: a blue car appeared. *That has to be the one Lotar is in,* she told herself.

Heart pounding, she braced herself, ready to leap onto the road to get the car to stop. But as she was about to jump forward—to her surprise and relief—the car came to a halt on its own where she most wanted it to stop.

* * *

With Poppy in front under the snakeskin, the mice, having worked their way through the orchard, reached the pump.

"I think we better stop and rest," said Poppy. "Maybe I can see where that raccoon went."

She came out from under the skin, climbed atop the pump pedestal, and studied Gray House. To her relief, she could see no raccoons. "The raccoon must have gone somewhere else," she called.

But as she continued to look at Gray House she realized not one mouse was in sight. That was unusual. She did see a pickup truck parked by the side of the road. A red car, too. And even as she took all that in, she observed a blue car coming along the road. It seemed to be the same car she had seen at the log house. What's more, the car slowed down and stopped right in front of Gray House.

"Is everything okay?" Basil called to Poppy.

"I'm not sure. I don't see any mice. That's strange. And there are cars in front of Gray House. Three of them. A truck and a red car. And a blue car just came. I think it's the one that was near that awful trap. It just stopped in front of Gray House. I think that means humans are there."

"What are they doing?"

"No idea."

"But no raccoons?" called Glory.

"Don't see them. But, to be safe, maybe we should keep under the snakeskin," said Poppy. "It scared the raccoons. Maybe it'll scare the people. I suggest we go around to the front of the house. With the snakeskin, it'll be easier than going up the steep back steps."

* * *

The three men inside the house heard the sound of the blue car stopping.

"That must be my clients," said Mr. Sonderson. He looked out the doorway. "What I'll be telling them is that the best thing about this place is how quiet and calm it is."

"About the only good thing," said the young man.

"And the closets," Mr. Gruffin said with a good-natured laugh. "Lots of closets."

The three men went out to the front porch to welcome the newcomers.

Dudley the dog kept barking and straining on his leash, wanting to get into the house.

"Easy boy," said Mr. Sonderson to the dog. "Stay. Nothing is going to happen."

CHAPTER 39

At Gray House

W HEN THE BLUE car came to a full stop, Susan picked up the trap, put her face close to it, and whispered to Ragweed, "Spaghetti, I'm only going away for a short time. I have to see the house. Don't go anywhere. I'll leave the windows open so you can have plenty of fresh air." She pushed a side button and this time the other back window opened.

"Sweetheart," said her father, "trust me, she can't go anywhere. You have her locked in that trap and you're going to keep the trap in the car, right?"

"I know. I wanted her to understand that I'll be back soon." With that, the girl set the trap down—with Ragweed inside—on the car's back seat. Then she opened the door, got out of the car, and walked across the road with her parents toward Gray House.

"Hi, there," called Mr. Sonderson, who was standing on

the front porch, his hand extended. "I'm Jack Sonderson. Real estate agent. Come right on in."

* * *

The mother raccoon saw the three people get out of the car. Then she watched as they went across the road toward Gray House and stepped onto the porch, where they were met by other people.

Where is Lotar? she asked herself. *Is he still in the car?*

* * *

Within the car, inside the cage, Ragweed looked around. He knew that all the people were gone. *Would they come back? The car was not moving. Was there some way that he could get out of the cage? Maybe this is my best chance.*

As he had many times before, he struggled to stretch the bars and lift the end flaps. It made no more difference than it had before.

He sat back. *Have to wait and see what happens.*

* * *

Under the car's back seat, Lotar also sensed that the car had stopped moving. He had heard the noise of the doors opening and slamming shut, though he was not sure what it meant. After listening to almost constant human talk since the car had started shaking and rumbling, he grasped he was no longer hearing any human voices.

Did those people go away? he asked himself.

He waited but nothing happened. And there were no more sounds to alarm him. *Maybe they left me alone.*

I wish someone would come and help me, he thought. The notion that no one would come filled him with anxiety.

What's going to happen to me?

Unable to wait anymore, he suddenly called out, "Mama! Where are you? Ragweed-mouse! Can you hear me? Guess what? I need your help again."

To his complete surprise what Lotar heard next was, "Dude, is that you?"

"Yes, it is me. Lotar. It is. It is. Is that you, Ragweed?"

Not only was Lotar excited to recognize Ragweed's voice, but he also heard, "Lotar, are you in there?"

The young raccoon could hardly believe it. That was his mother's voice. The two most important voices in the world—his mother's voice and his best friend's voice—both telling him that they were near and ready to rescue him.

Excited and relieved, Lotar crawled out from under the car seat. When he stood up on his hind legs, the first thing he saw was the trap and that inside the trap was Ragweed.

"Ragweed," he cried. "You came to help me. And you found my mama again. Thank you. That proves you love me and I love you."

Ragweed looked at the raccoon with astonishment. "How come you're here? And can't you see, I'm the one who needs help."

"Why?"

"It's this trap I'm in. You need to get me out. Like, use

your claws and, you know, see if you can open one of the end flaps."

Lotar climbed up on the seat and made some fumbling pulls at the cage. "It won't open," he said.

"Tell me about it," said Ragweed.

"Lotar," came a call from outside. "Did you hear me? Answer me. Are you in there?"

Lotar hurried to the window, climbed up, and looked out. Sitting on the ground he saw his mother. "Hello, Mama. Guess who's here?"

"I don't care who's there," she said. "I need you to come out of that car right now and come to me."

"I can't."

"Why?"

"Because my best friend Ragweed-mouse is here. He's in a trap and can't get out."

"*Who* did you say is there?"

"Ragweed-mouse. My best friend. The one you threw away."

"How did he get in there?"

"He came to help me because he loves me and he's brave and now he needs *my* help."

"I don't care anything about him," said the mother raccoon. "I want you to get out of there. Now. We need to go home."

Lotar shook his head. "No, I can't. My friend helped me. Now I have to help him. Only I can't open the thing he's in. Would you please come in here and help me get him out? You have stronger claws than I do."

The big raccoon sighed, looked around, and when she saw there was nothing to endanger her, she leaped up, grabbed hold of the car window edge, drew herself up, and then dropped down inside the car onto the car's back seat.

Ragweed, seeing the huge raccoon come into the car, and remembering what she did the last time they were together, shrank down.

The big raccoon put her face against the cage. "What are you doing in there?" she demanded of Ragweed.

"Dude, I promise, I don't want to be in here. But I can't get out. How about, you know, helping me out?"

"If I do, are you going to take my boy away again?"

"I never did take him away. Trust me, it's him that keeps coming after me. You're welcome to keep him. Forever."

The mother raccoon turned to Lotar. "If I get this creature out of this box do you absolutely promise to stay away from him and come home with me?"

"I want you to get him out."

"How do we do that?"

"He said you have to open that part," said Lotar, pointing to the trap's end flap.

The mother raccoon, poking and prying, studied the trap intently. She sat back. "Okay. I think I can do it." She flexed her long claws.

With that, she flipped up the U-bar that held one of the trapdoors down. That was easy to do. Next, she pushed all her claws under the flap, lifted it a bit, then, with a grunt, pulled the flap entirely up, even as she called, "It's open."

"Hurrah," called Lotar and he clapped his paws.

Ragweed saw his chance. He ran out of the cage. Once he was out, the raccoon let the flap shut with a sharp *snap*.

"I did it," cried Lotar with joy. "I freed Ragweed-mouse."

On the car seat, free of the trap, it took Ragweed only seconds to realize he was indeed completely free. *Dude,* he told himself, *yank yourself out of here.*

He looked for the best way to go. On one side of the car seat sat Lotar and the mother raccoon, effectively blocking the way to that window. Ragweed turned. The other window was open and the way was clear.

"See you," he called, ran across the seat, and quickly crawled up the side of the door to the open window. When he looked out, he saw a building.

It seemed familiar.

I know that place. That's where Poppy comes from. Gray House. Maybe she got home. I should say goodbye to her before I take off.

With that thought, Ragweed leaped from the car, dropping to the ground. Once there, he looked up and down, saw that there was no danger, and raced across the road.

Once across, Ragweed looked into the front yard of Gray House. It was deserted. *That's weird,* he thought. *Last time I came here the place was crowded with mice. What's going on?*

He continued forward, but as he approached the front porch, he saw a dog. The dog was straining on a leash, barking loudly, trying to get into the house.

Fearful of the dog, Ragweed halted. Then he saw that the dog was being held back by that leash. *If Poppy is in the house she may be in trouble,* he thought. Measuring with his eyes how far the dog could reach, Ragweed darted around him and ran into the house.

* * *

Lotar, dismayed that Ragweed had jumped out of the car, clawed his way to the open window and looked out. He was just in time to see Ragweed scoot across the road and head for Gray House.

"Ragweed, don't leave me again," he called. "I rescued you. You're my best friend. Don't go away."

Ragweed kept going.

"Ragweed," shouted Lotar. "Wait for me!"

Remembering how he had jumped from the train, and knowing he could do so safely, Lotar leaped.

* * *

"Oh no!" cried Poppy to the mice behind her. She was still under the snakeskin—as were all the others. They had come round the corner of Gray House. "I just saw a raccoon. It's heading for the house. Come on. We need to chase it away."

* * *

"Lotar," cried the mother raccoon from the blue car. "Where are you going? You promised that if I freed that mouse you would come home with me."

Furious, she crawled up to the open window. Perched on the sill she looked out and saw Lotar heading for Gray House.

"Come back, you foolish raccoon," she called. But when he did not stop, she sprang down to the road. Determined to bring him back, she headed for the house.

* * *

As Lotar reached the front yard of Gray House he heard something coming around the house. He stopped, looked, and could hardly believe what he saw: It was that snake moving round the corner of the house. *It's followed me,* was his instant, fearful thought. *It's still coming after me.*

Terribly frightened, he went up the Gray House steps and raced across the front porch. Seeing the doorway was open, he ran right by the startled dog.

* * *

Dudley, seeing the raccoon run by, gave a yelp and lunged forward. He did it with such sudden power, the post to which his leash had been tied broke free. Completely unrestrained, Dudley dashed into the house in pursuit of Lotar.

* * *

As the mama raccoon reached the far side of the road, she simultaneously saw three things: a snake, Lotar rushing into the house, and a dog chasing after him. Her only thought was, *My boy is in horrible danger. I have to save him.*

With that, she raced toward the house.

* * *

When Poppy came around to the front of the house, she stopped. First, she had seen one raccoon head for Gray House. Then she saw and heard the dog, barking feverishly, break free, leap forward, and also race into the house. Now she saw a second raccoon. She watched, horrified, as it scrambled up onto the porch and then inside.

"Guys," she called, "I just saw two raccoons and an angry dog go into Gray House."

"What are they doing there?" asked Primrose.

"Don't know, but our family probably needs help. Maybe we can scare them all out with this snakeskin."

"Cool," shouted Toadflax. "Let's do it."

"Follow me," cried Poppy. In moments, she and the rest of the mice were on the porch and heading through the open doorway.

CHAPTER 40

Inside Gray House

"Yes," THE REAL estate agent was saying to Susan's parents, who were standing in the largest room of the house, "the house does require a great deal of work, but I can assure you it'll make a lovely, quiet home."

Susan, bored with the talk, walked into the front room and moved toward the doorway. That was when she saw Ragweed run into the house through the front doorway.

"Spaghetti," cried the girl. "You got lonely and came after me." She rushed forward to catch the mouse.

Ragweed, seeing the girl come toward him, hands extended as if wanting to snare him, ran away as fast as he could.

Lotar, fleeing the snake, ran into the house and shot right past the girl.

"Mommy! Daddy!" Susan shouted, "there's an animal in the house and he's trying to catch Spaghetti."

Ragweed headed for the main room.

So did Lotar.

So did Susan.

Now it was Dudley the dog who burst forward, trying to catch Lotar.

"And," the real estate agent in the main room was saying, "as you can see, this house has many closets." As he spoke he opened one of the closet doors. When he did, forty-five terrified mice gazed up at him. One look at the human standing there and, squealing and squeaking, they poured out of the closet and began to search for safety in all directions.

Susan entered the room, and seeing all the mice, cried, "Mommy, Daddy, look. The house is full of Spaghetti's family."

As she spoke, the mother raccoon, in pursuit of Lotar, rushed into the house. "Lotar, come here!" she called.

Lotar glanced back, only to see the barking dog chasing him. He searched for somewhere to go and saw only one place. He ran to Susan and hugged her leg.

Susan began to scream.

The dog, standing in front of her, barked furiously.

Ragweed, catching sight of an old hat in a corner,

climbed to the crown where he could watch what was happening.

"Dudley," cried Mr. Sonderson. "Come right over here! Get in this closet." He pulled open a door. Though the dog did not come, a hundred more mice poured out of the closet and scattered in all directions.

The mother raccoon, seeing that her boy was being attacked by the dog, raced forward and leaped upon the dog's back and gripped him tightly with her strong claws. Dudley, taken by surprise, started yelping and began to run around in circles, trying to shake the raccoon off.

Mice were everywhere, squealing and shrieking, attempting to get away and find safety.

"Dudley," cried Mr. Sonderson. "Come here, boy." He, too, chased after the dog.

Mr. Gruffin and his assistant were trying to help Mr. Sonderson corner the dog, while also attempting to pull off the mother raccoon.

"Let's see if we can get that dog in here!" Mr. Gruffin shouted to his assistant. He pulled open another closet door.

Fifty more mice ran out of the closet and began their own frantic search for safety.

Now it was Susan's parents who rushed to their daughter's aid and attempted to pluck off Lotar. Lotar, panicky, clung to her leg. The girl kept shouting, "Get it off! Get it off!"

The next moment, Poppy and the other mice, under the snakeskin, walked into the room.

Seeing the snake, everyone in the room froze.

It was Susan who shouted, "A snake just came in!"

"Out!" Susan's father shouted. "Everybody out of here."

It was Susan's mother who grabbed Lotar, pulled him from her daughter's leg, and flipped him across the room. Then she took hold of her daughter's hand and fairly dragged her out of the room and the house, not stopping until they reached the car. They jumped in and were followed by Susan's father.

The mother raccoon, seeing that Lotar was standing alone in the middle of the room, confused and not sure where to turn, rushed up to him. "Come on, baby," she said. "Follow me. No more nonsense."

Lotar did not resist. The two raccoons raced toward the back of the house and the only way open to them, reached the rear porch, kept going into the orchard, and were soon out of sight.

At the same time, Mr. Gruffin and his assistant hurried out the front doorway.

Mr. Sonderson, holding tightly to his dog's collar, went after them. They stood together in front of Gray House. They watched the blue car drive away.

"I have to think," said Mr. Gruffin, "those folks are not going to buy the house."

"I doubt anyone will," said Mr. Sonderson.

"I'd be happy to knock it down," said the young man.

"Call me if you need anything," said Mr. Gruffin, and he and his assistant headed for the pickup truck.

Mr. Sonderson pulled up the For Sale sign and flung it in his car. Then he and Dudley got in and drove off.

* * *

The blue car was moving quickly down the Tar Road.

"Are we going to live in that house?" asked Susan.

"I think," said her mother, "there are too many other creatures already living there."

"But what about Spaghetti?" said the girl, bursting into tears.

"Sweetheart, you are going to have to get another friend," said her father.

"What . . . what kind of animal was it that hugged my leg?"

"A raccoon, I think?"

"He was cute. Can I have one of those?"

"We can think about it," said Susan's father.

"What we need," suggested Susan's mother, "is a nice, calm picnic."

* * *

In Gray House, Ragweed looked across the floor of the room and saw the mice throw off the snakeskin.

"Poppy," he cried. "Am I glad to see you."

Poppy, in return, said, "Ragweed, how did you get here?"

It was at that moment that Lungwort emerged from his boot. He looked around and saw hundreds of mice standing around, looking befuddled. Seeing Farmer Lamout's straw hat in a corner, he climbed up and, from the crown he cried, "All right, family. Please, gather in close. I need to tell you what to do."

* * *

Somewhere in the middle of Dimwood Forest, under the mound of rocks, Lotar snuggled up close to his mama.

"Do you think," Lotar asked, "that Ragweed-mouse is lost?"

"I'm sure he'll be fine."

"He was my friend."

"You'll make lots of friends."

"Mama . . ."

"What?"

"You're my best friend."

"And you're mine. Now go to sleep."

"Okay," said Lotar and that's what he did.

CHAPTER 41

The Party

AT GRAY HOUSE that evening the mice had a grand party. Toadflax had taken up a position by the side of the road. His job was to watch for any returning humans. So far Gray House was safe.

Assembled on the front porch, the whole family exchanged stories about what had happened. A hesitant Poppy was called upon to relate her adventures. Then came Basil, who spoke of what happened to him, and all those who went out across Long Meadow to rescue Poppy. Finally, Poppy insisted that Ragweed tell about everything that had happened to him, from the time he met the baby raccoon on the train, to the moment he returned to Gray House.

By the time the tales were done, it was dark. There were stars in the sky over Bannock Hill, and closer to earth, fireflies sparked in earnest.

Ragweed and Poppy sat close together.

"Thank you for trying to save me," Poppy said to Ragweed.

"Dude," Ragweed said to her, "thanks for trying to save me. Hey, I was thinking of going back to a city. But I think, if you don't mind, I'll be a country mouse in a house. At least for a while. That hill over there . . . ," said Ragweed, pointing across the way. A full moon bathed its summit in yellow light.

"It's called Bannock Hill," said Poppy.

"Looks like that top of it would be a good place to dance. What do you think?"

For a brief moment, Poppy closed her eyes. "Maybe," she said. "I need to be home a while."

Ragweed touched his earring to make sure it was there, then stood up in front of all the mice and said, "Dudes, I have a song to teach you. It's my family's favorite song."

Standing in front of all the mice he sang:

"A mouse will a-roving go,
Along wooded paths and pebbled ways
To places high and places low,
Where birds do sing 'neath sunny rays,
For the world is full of mice, oh!
For the world is full of mice, oh!"

He went on to sing the second verse:

"A mouse will a-roving go,
By highways, byways and long wooded trails
To forests; cities. Rain or snow,
Not bothered by cats, or the smallest snails
For the world is full of mice, oh!
For the world is full of mice, oh!"

Finally, he got all the mice to join in and sing the last verse:

"A mouse will a-roving go,
Over hills and along the tumbling creeks
To climb the rocks and swim each flow.
No cares for time—hours, days, or weeks,
It's the joy of life that every mouse seeks,
For the world is full of mice, oh!
For the world is full of mice, oh!"

A Mouse Will A-Roving Go

Words by Avi
Music by Shaun Wolf Wortis

copyright Avi

To hear the song go to http://mousesong.com.

Acknowledgments

Over the twenty-five years during which the seven Poppy books were created, there have been three editors.

Richard Jackson edited *Poppy*.

Elise Howard edited *Ragweed, Poppy and Rye, Ereth's Birthday, Poppy's Return, Poppy and Ereth*.

Alexandra Cooper edited *Ragweed and Poppy*.

It is to these talented folks' credit that the books share the same spirit, humor, and personality, even as they are all different. Writer and artist acknowledge our great debt.

Over the years we, writer and artist, have grown older. It is our fondest hope that the books have stayed young.

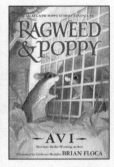
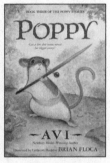
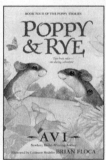